Trapper's Moon

by

Gini Rifkin

Trapper's Moon

Cover Art by *The Wild Rose Press, Inc.*

The Wild Rose Press, Inc.
PO Box 708
Adams Basin, NY 14410-0708
Visit us at www.thewildrosepress.com

Publishing History
First Cactus Rose Edition, 2019
Print ISBN 978-1-5092-2990-1
Digital ISBN 978-1-5092-2991-8

Published in the United States of America

Remaining at her back, and seeming to understand, he rested his hands upon her shoulders.

"I'm not giving up on us, Blind Deer. I can wait."

When she turned her head to glance back at him, he kissed her cheek, and then reaching for one of her hands, he drew her closer to the window. "The moon is so big tonight it reminds me of a Trapper's Moon."

Blind Deer squinted up at the sky, and although she would never know the patterns formed by the twinkling bits of light, her shortcoming did not stifle her curiosity for the world around her.

"What exactly is a Trapper's Moon?" She was glad they pursued a subject other than the history of her love life, or lack thereof. And she enjoyed hearing about anything to do with Saka'am, the moon.

"It comes in February, and it's a formidable sight—big and bright, like a golden plum, ripe for the picking. A body feels he might reach out and touch it if he could but climb a bit higher up into the heavens. So bright does it shine, if the rivers are thawed, a trapper can walk his lines all night long using the light it gives off to show him the way."

Blind Deer watched Kade's face as he spoke. His strong profile and earnest expression revealed his great love for the land and the wilderness. A handsome and noble face, one she fancied she would have been content to grow old beside.

Kudos for Gini Rifkin and…

Dedication

In memory of Gary, my mountain man

~

Thank you again to
The Wild Rose Press and Amanda Barnett

Author's Note...

Before the pioneers and wagon trains, before the cowboys and herds of cattle, there were the Mountain Men—taming, exploring, and oftentimes dying in the New Frontier.

Many were trappers, and they needed a practical way to get their coveted beaver hides to the East Coast. Between the years 1825-1840 the rendezvous came into being. These gatherings were an amazing confluence of humanity bringing together the good, the bad, and the you name it, crossing paths head-on, some by design, some by accident.

French, English, Americans, and Native tribes met in the summer for a mere few weeks of organized chaos, friendly competition, and serious trading. Entrepreneurs brought supplies from back East to exchange for the hides used to fashion haute couture in the form of top hats and coats for high society folks. But all was not fun and games.

The American fur trade companies were at odds with the Hudson's Bay Company, owned by the British and known as the HBC. Some of the French and Indians were at odds with all who came to invade their territory. It was a tumultuous era when telling friend from foe could mean the difference between life and death. And loyalty, as well as knowing how to live free and in partnership with the Stony Mountains, was all that kept a man or woman alive.

~*~

For your reference, a glossary of terms is listed at the back of the book. Waugh!

Prologue

Summer, 1833, St. Louis, Missouri

A smile, cold and cruel, slid across old lady Dalrymple's face. "One way or another, girl, your heathen soul is gonna be redeemed. Maybe a little time in the dark will help you to see the light." The woman disappeared, her laughter fading as the door to the root cellar slammed shut.

The blackness descended mercilessly, complete, and dark as a tomb, which seemed fitting enough as Reverend Dalrymple and his wife wished to kill the *Red Spirit* inside her.

Pounding on the unyielding wood and howling at the top of her lungs, her rage and misery echoed around her. Then she jerked to a halt, palms pressed flat against the roughhewn planks. Even if they could hear her, no one at the boarding school would come to her rescue. Only Cook showed her a modicum of compassion—the rest either feared or hated her.

Easing away from the door, she groped her way around the dank enclosure. Coming upon a sack of potatoes, she climbed atop the burlap-covered mound—at least it was warmer than the cold earthen floor. Still shaking with anger, she wrenched off the too-tight shoes her captors forced her to wear and tore at the dress and camisole restricting her breathing.

How had it all gone so wrong? The Iroquois people, friend to her tribe, promised the Black Robes were kind, harboring no cruelty in their hearts. But these missionaries were not Black Robes. These missionaries knew only harsh ways. She must find her people and tell them the truth.

Because her mother was a white woman, they acted as if they were obliged to save her. But she knew better—it was for the money. If she bent to their will, she would be a great success story, an example of how their religion redeemed her from her wicked Indian ways. People would pay to look at her, or to sit and drink tea in her presence.

When her mother read verse from her special book, the words spoke of kindness and of living in peace with all creatures. These people invoked their God with spite and malice, with no concern for the life she had lived or the family she had loved for sixteen winters.

A scurrying noise sounded in the corner. Reaching for her knife, she grasped only a fistful of calico cloth—they had left her armed with nothing but memories.

The air seemed to thicken and press down upon her, and the quiet roared in her ears. Refusing to cry, she shivered in the darkness. Her stomach knotted with fear, and her mouth turned dry as the bread they fed her.

The pounding of her heart shook her body like the once familiar cadence of the drums, and rocking to and fro, she chanted the prayers her grandfather had taught her. She smelled the woodsmoke, felt the wind on her face, and the remembrance of another time and place gave her strength.

The Christians had stolen her tack belt and hide dress. They had cut off her hair and called her Belinda Dearborn. They tried to destroy everything that made her who and what she was. But as long as she drew breath she would never forget.

Her name was Blind Deer—and she was of The People.

Chapter One

Three long years later. St. Louis, May 1836

If they knew how she suffered, they would come to her rescue. But her family didn't know, and they hadn't come. Tonight, Blind Deer had a chance to save herself.

If her plan worked, she would no longer be their slave. Her hands would no longer grow numb in the freezing winters as she made lye soap or washed windows. And her back would no longer ache in the blistering summers as she tended their garden and scrubbed their floors.

Tonight could not come soon enough.

Glancing in both directions, making sure no one was in sight, she crept down the back hall and at the west end scrambled up the rickety ladder to the attic. While the rest of the household swarmed about like angry bees in preparation for this evening's brush with royalty, Blind Deer intended to search the eaves of the house for the clothing stolen from her when she'd arrived. She'd heard talk that the Reverend and his wife had stored the remnants of her heathen past somewhere up here. Why? She couldn't imagine—perhaps as a depraved souvenir.

She rummaged through a nearby duffle—nothing in there but white people clothes. Odd they hadn't burned her pagan trappings. They were always preaching about the fires of hell. Instead, they'd stored them, if the rumors were true, in the highest room in the house. The one closest to their heaven. That thought kindled a smile.

She flung back the lid to a large steamer trunk. Behold, there they were—along with pieces of other women's clothing—Indian women of various tribes. Apparently, she was not the first to be held captive in this house of misery. Wondering what had become of the other females, she bundled their few worldly possessions together with her own and crept back down to the floor below.

The sleeping quarters, hot in the summer and cold in the winter, had been partitioned off into several smaller rooms. Female servants, orphans, and schoolgirl charity cases—like her—shared the poorly ventilated accommodations. Slipping away to her allotted space, she secreted the items beneath her pallet—and just in time.

"Belinda Dearborn. Front and center. Now."

Blind Deer smoothed the wrinkles from the flouncy dress they insisted she wear and headed toward the voice that harried her dreams. Like any good warrior, she had learned to pick her battles. Today she pretended what she wore didn't matter, and in truth it did not—as long as doing so meant keeping alive what was inside of her. Besides, her cooperation lulled them into thinking they had won, which gave her the advantage of surprise, as well as access to the guests who visited here.

As she stepped forward for inspection, Reverend Dalrymple's wife eyed her from head to toe. "You'd best smile and behave yourself tonight, missy, if you know what's good for you." Visciously grabbing Blind Deer by one arm, the older woman emphasized her threat. "Lord Seton has promised a large donation to the mission and boarding school. You are our example as to how his money will be put to good use. Are you listening to me?" The painful grip tightened.

Blind Deer wretched her arm free. "Yes, I understand. You have my word. I will not fail to impress Lord Seton." *Although not in the manner you are expecting.*

Mrs. Dalrymple cocked her head to one side, and her eyes narrowed as if she suspected skullduggery. Blind Deer quickly cast her gaze downward in the submissive manner to which the older woman was partial.

"If you misbehave, you'll feel the lash. It still has your dried blood on it. We keep it handy, just for you. Well, don't stand there dawdling. Go to the kitchen and help Cook. And don't get dirty. If there is one spot on your dress, you will know my wrath."

Nothing new there. The woman was always embittered about something or someone.

Hiking up her skirts immodestly high, Blind Deer strutted down the hall in the most unladylike manner she could envision. The expected horrified shriek and reprimand erupted in her wake. Rounding a corner, she settled into a proper walk and headed for the kitchen.

The aroma of roast pork turning on the spit danced around the room, hand in hand with the delicious smell of fresh baked breads, mushroom pie, and Cook's famous fruit tarts. It was a banquet rarely seen within these walls, and more food than Blind Deer remembered ever seeing at one time in one room.

"It's about time. Get to it, girl. The pots and pans be piled to the ceiling." Cook, with her hands on her hips, stood in the center of the kitchen, master of all she surveyed as she called out orders.

Blind Deer plunged her hands into the awaiting soapy water. Lord Seton, tonight's guest of honor, would surely be impressed by such an array of food.

The thought of meeting the man both frightened and excited her. Earlier in the month, while cleaning the hearth in an adjoining room, she'd overheard a conversation between this British aristocrat and the Reverend and Mrs. Dalrymple.

With ill intent, the nefarious couple successfully endured several missionary excursions to the west. Their visitor, unaware of the dubious methods used to garner money and obtain the hired help, came seeking the Reverend's advice regarding the best route heading in the same direction.

They'd spoken of other matters as well.

The British nobleman, a hero from the Napoleonic war, fancied himself a great explorer. And being an ardent admirer of American folk heroes and the Red Indians, he declared when he reached the West that he intended to shoot a grizzly bear in honor of Hugh Glass, and he yearned to meet an Indian chief, and spend the night in a tipi. She would gladly introduce him to her Grandfather—assuming her plan worked.

Cook shoved another pot into her hands, and Blind Deer dutifully scraped and scrubbed at the dried-on mess. Would this evening be her salvation or her undoing?

****

The hour grew late. Still the three people in the

dining room lingered over the extravagant meal.

Dressed in full Indian regalia, Blind Deer was too nervous to be tired as she hid in the hallway waiting to serve dessert. Although she had grown taller, being half starved most of the time she hadn't grown any larger around, and thankfully the clothing still fit.

Red faced and even more overworked than usual, Cook finally appeared rolling forward the little cart holding the sweets. The older woman positioned the trolley beside the doorway, and as their gazes locked, the expression on the portly woman's face transformed from wide-eyed to mirthful. Heading back the way she'd come, Cook shook her head and gave a hearty laugh.

Hopefully, Lord Seton's reaction would be of a more serious nature.

Adjusting the quilled dangles in her hair, Blind Deer resettled the tack belt around her waist and straightened the borrowed knife sheath, strike-a-light bag, and awl case attached to it. What had become of the Indian women who had lovingly made these personal items? When she'd dared to ask another servant, she had been told they had run away, never to be seen again. Did they fare well, or had they died for trying to escape the clutches of the missionaries?

"Belinda's deliverance is a true miracle." Pride and arrogance rode Reverend Dalrymple's words, and at the sound of the white name by which they called her, Blind Deer came to attention and listened more closely. "A glorious transformation, done gratis on our part, of course." Apparently, her labors were worth nothing in trade.

"Such a lovely obedient girl," the wife added, the

blatant lie dripping with sweetness to rival the confections waiting to be served. "But you must judge for yourself, Sir Reginald. Belinda, dear, you may bring the dessert now."

Shoulders back, and steeling herself for what was to come, Blind Deer maneuvered the cart into the dining room.

The reverend's eyes bugged out like a toad being squeezed too hard, and he turned whiter than the Sunday shirts she scrubbed and bleached for him.

Old lady Dalrymple, mouth agape and working like a landed fish, rose halfway out of her chair. Recovering quickly, she eased back onto the seat, fire burning in her eyes. "I'm sorry, Lord Seton. There has obviously been some mistake."

"Nonsense. Come along, my dear. Let me look at your costume." Blind Deer gritted her teeth at the term costume but smiled and stepped closer. "Where are you from? What is your tribe?" His eyes sparkled with interest as well as amusement.

"I am of The People, from the Bitterroot."

"And how is it you speak American so well? And my word, you have green eyes."

"My father is Salish, but my mother is a white woman. She taught me your language—and I miss her terribly." Although true, she added the last to play upon his sympathy. "My father rescued my mother from the Siksika, the Blackfoot Indians."

"The Blackfoot... By Jove. I've heard they're a fearsome lot, and on the bellicose side, prone to warring and raiding and all manner of unspeakable mischief. Your mother was fortunate to be liberated from the dastardly scoundrels. What in Heaven's name was she doing out West?"

"Following her heart." *That's what Mother always said when we asked that question.*

"What her mother thought or did is of no importance," the Reverend declared.

"On the contrary," Lord Seton countered. "Part of my reason for exploring your country is to learn about the people, and what makes them who they are. King William is working to restore relations between England and America, and he has championed my undertaking most vigorously. Pray, go on, child."

As the Reverend and Mrs. Dalrymple retreated into angry silence, Blind Deer studied Lord Seton. He was by no means a young man, but he hadn't quite gone paunchy since leaving the military. His mouth was not generous, but he seemed quick to smile, and his clear gray eyes offered the unwavering gaze of a man with seemingly nothing to hide. At his nod of encouragement, and with all the animation she could muster, Blind Deer recounted the facts as they had been told to her.

"My mother was born right here, in St. Louis. Her father, a purveyor of medicine, was determined to bring the white man's cures to the West. To that end he and his family along with a small band of likeminded souls set out to do so."

She couldn't resist glancing pointedly toward the Reverend and his wife. "I'm told they also brought the message of the white God. But they did not beat their religion into those who came to them—nor beat the devil out of those who resisted." Old Lady Dalrymple averted her gaze first. The reverend held on a little longer.

Seeming not to notice the conflict, Lord Seton turned sideways in his chair and leaned forward as if eager to hear more. "And what happened next? Is that when they ran into the infamous Blackfoot savages?" Being a military man, he seemed fascinated with the battle aspect of her story rather than her family history, so like any good storyteller she followed his lead.

"Oh yes. On that terrible day, the Blackfoot warriors swooped down upon the harmless group, and all were killed in a horrific battle—except my mother and her best friend. They were captured and led away, each with a rope around their neck. Then my brave father appeared—spear in one hand, war club in the other. He and his companions fought long and hard, driving off the Blackfoot horde. Then my father scooped up one of the bedraggled white women and carried her away to make her his bride."

"And she willingly stayed with this warrior and his tribe?" The man sounded incredulous.

"Why of course. My father and mother love one another very much—and very often. My three brothers and I are proof of that."

Lord Seton slapped one thigh and gave a hearty laugh at her insinuation.

The reverend gained his feet, toppling his chair over in the process. "Enough." He pointed a finger in her direction, "You will leave this room immediately— to be dealt with later."

She dared to glare back at him. This was her only chance to speak with Lord Seton—her only chance for freedom.

"I can read and write your language, sir." She blurted out the words, gripping the handle of the cart

11

with cold hands. All appeared stunned at her declaration. Had she made a mistake in revealing her greatest weapon?

Along with speaking the language, her mother had taught her both of these skills at an early age. But here, to aggravate her teachers and old lady Dalrymple, she pretended otherwise. And when they were not watching, she borrowed and read nearly every one of the donated books in the library. Those precious tomes fed her soul and mind many times better than the scraps of food they threw at her to feed her body.

She would miss the books—her only friends.

The reverend unclenched his jaw and appeared about to speak.

"I also have many maps in my head," she added, cutting him off. The atlas she'd discovered held drawings of 18th Century Europe, hardly useful to Lord Seton, but she'd gained a feel for these types of renderings, wouldn't such knowledge be helpful?

At wit's end, she wracked her brain for a means of convincing him to take her along on his journey to the west. *Keep talking, keep talking. He liked the story about the battle. Tell him about the other explorers.*

"Long ago, Lewis and Clark visited the land of my people—the elders were children then, but they still remember. They still have many tales to tell."

"Lewis and Clark." For a moment, Sir Reginald's eyes glowed with faraway visions, and he whispered the names with reverence usually reserved for deities. "I've read their journals—their expedition was extraordinary, legendary. And I've heard the tales of Beckwourth, and Fremont."

"And Charbonneau and Sacagawea." Daring to say

more, she slipped in the noteworthy names. "Like the Shoshone girl who led Lewis and Clark to the far side of the mountains, if you take me along with you, I will help you in your endeavors."

Why didn't he say something? Tears threatened, but she balled her hands into fists and refused to cry. She was a warrior, the granddaughter of a great chief. She would show no fear. Meeting his stern gaze, she stood tall and unflinching.

Finally, the man who held her future—possibly her life—in his hands, turned to face her captors.

"Reverend, Mrs. Dalrymple, I have a proposition for you."

Chapter Two

The High Uintas, June, 1836

"Shoot again, Kade. Somethin's still a movin' in them there pinion pine."

Kade McCauley took aim in the direction Tucket, his friend and partner, indicated. The blast from the flintlock rifle filled the air, and sulfurous smoke drifted through shafts of morning sunlight. An unsettling whimper came from his intended target, followed by a sudden stillness.

"Damnedest thing I ever did see or hear tell of," Tucket declared as both men reloaded their longrifles. "Mountain men skirmishin' with other mountain men. It ain't natural. It's hard enough stayin' alive out here fightin' the occasional Indian let alone each other."

"Stop talking and listen," Kade ordered, straining to hear signs of life from their attackers. The warble of a meadowlark floated on the breeze, and the buzz of insects hummed in counterpoint, but nothing sinister broke the mood.

Hunkering down lower behind the ridge of rocks, he glanced over at their mules and thanked the Lord they remained tethered in the aspen grove to the south. The last of the supplies, and all of the hides they had taken during the season, were in those packs. Those stalwart critters were transporting the future of two men.

The big dog at his side leaned against him and sniffed the air, eager to be on the move. "Easy, Maggie," Kade cautioned. "We'll take a look-see in a minute." People often thought the name Maggie a curious choice for such a fierce animal resembling a blue-eyed overgrown coyote. But he'd raised her since she was a pup and knew her softer side.

"My bad knee's a killin' me, Kade," the older man groused, rubbing the offending part of his anatomy. "I think I'd rather stand up and be shot than tolerate this contortion of a position much longer."

"All right... I guess it seems quiet enough. Let's circle around and check things out. I'll take the left." He added the last bit out of habit, not because he needed to. He always took the left, and his partner knew he would. It just never hurt to make sure everyone understood the plan when your life depended on it.

As Tucket headed off in the opposite direction, Kade crouched low to the ground and edged around the stony outcropping. When no movement or gun fire erupted, he stood taller and advanced forward. His moccasin-clad feet whispered on the dry earth, and the green branches of new foliage snagged at the worn fringes on his buckskins.

The smell of gun powder still hung in the air, mixing oddly with the sweetness of summer. Too bad he couldn't enjoy the warmth of the sun without having to worry about his backside.

Nearing the remains of a burned-out cabin, he circled the rubble. Behind a pile of rock, once a hearth and chimney, he found two men—they were dead, and based on appearances working for the British. Each one displayed the Hudson's Bay Company emblem on his capote and accouterments.

The nearby foliage rustled. Kade took note, gun raised at the ready. Then he relaxed. It was Tucket, striding his way with that uneven gait of his. "What'd you find?" he asked, lowering his rifle to cradle it in the crook of his arm.

"One dead man and a woman."

"A woman?" The thought of a female seemed a foreign idea. He tried not to think about them during the long winters in the high country. "What would a woman be doing out here? Where is she?"

"Yes, a woman. I don't know, and she's over there in them pine. You must have got her with your last shot."

Kade clenched his jaw, and his stomach constricted. "I never hurt a woman before in my life, and now you're telling me I killed one."

"Stop a whinin', she ain't dead. Bet it was her makin' that hurt rabbit noise we heard."

With relief calming his senses, Kade followed Tucket toward a little clearing—Maggie at his heels.

"So far I caught two of their horses and tied them up over yonder." His partner gave a nod in the other direction as he led the way. "I also heard a commotion in the woods. It's possible one of them got away."

Kade didn't like the sound of that. He glanced around but saw and heard nothing out of the ordinary.

The female lay on her side, crumpled on the ground like a doll abandoned by a thoughtless child. The earth near her left shoulder was shiny with blood. Kade's stomach knotted again at the sight of her body, silent and unmoving, her slim frame seemingly so fragile and helpless.

"She's dressed like an Indian, but under all the dirt I swear she looks like a white woman. What do you think, Kade?"

Kneeling at her side, Kade eased the girl onto her back and raised the sleeve of her leather dress, exposing her shoulder. "If we don't stop the bleeding," he muttered, continuing his examination, "it won't make much difference what she is."

Tucket drew closer and peered down at the young woman. "Looks like the lead went clean through, right on the edge and not too deep."

"Missed the bone. Thank providence." The words Kade offered were more to reassure himself than to inform his friend.

Freeing his patch knife, Kade cut off the cleanest piece of material he could find on his riverboat shirt. He then folded the fabric and wrapped it around the girl's upper arm. Jerking a couple of long fringes free from the seam in Tucket's leather pants, he used them to secure the makeshift bandage in place. After the long winter, there weren't many leather thongs left from which to choose.

The bleeding lessened dramatically. Relieved, Kade sat back on his heels measuring the steady rise and fall of the young woman's chest. Then shifting his gaze, he studied the remainder of her slim form.

She seemed a patchwork of cultures. Her hair, braided Indian style and decorated with quill work, had a noticeable curl. It was an odd cross between black and brown, as if undecided as to what shade it wanted to be. From her buckskins, it was impossible to tell which tribe she favored. Her three-hide dress and leggings were Flathead, her strike-a-light bag and awl case Cheyenne, and her tack belt Iroquois. She looked like she'd plum raided every trading post between St. Louis and the Sweetwater.

Kade pressed his fingers to the side of her throat to check her pulse, and his forearm brushed across the front of her buckskins. The hard wear and tear indicated by her clothing seemed contrary to the softness he felt beneath them.

"She should do fine unless infection sets in. I wonder what she was doing with a Hudson's Bay scouting party."

"Hard to say." Tucket pondered. "What we gonna do with her, Kade?"

"Guess we don't have much choice. We sure can't leave her here."

"I'll round up the spotted horse rigged Indian style," Tucket volunteered.

As the older man circled and crooned and clicked his tongue in an attempt to outsmart the painted cayuse pony, Maggie cautiously crept forward to inspect their unconscious patient. She gave a sniff and rubbed her cold wet nose against the female's pale cheek.

The young woman's eyes fluttered opened, then widened as she stared at Kade. He stared back, transfixed by the color of a forest in springtime. When her gaze settled on Maggie, she blanched even more, but didn't move a muscle, and the stoic defiance in her expression somehow made her seem even more delicate.

"Don't be scared, miss." Kade took care to remain unmoving—unthreatening. "We aren't about to hurt you. Well, at least not anymore. What I mean to say is

I'm sorry I shot you." He grimaced and searched for more suitable words.

She continued to watch him, not reacting at all.

"Can you understand me?"

No answer.

He reached for his canteen gourd to offer her a drink, and she shrank back, even at this mere action. "I just thought you might like to wet your dry," he explained. "You look a might parched."

She eyed the gourd and licked her lips but made no other movement.

He held his empty hand out, palm up, and smiled at her. With the other, he offered the gourd.

"You're thirsty—here."

She glanced from his hand to the offered water and back to his face. He thought it might be easier to convince his dog to eat porcupine than to get this female to take one swallow of water. "You don't need to be so stubborn," he coaxed softly.

Relenting, she tried to sit up, but unable to gain leverage, she fell back with a moan.

Without thinking, he eased forward. Encouraged when she didn't shy away, he helped her to prop herself up on her good arm and carefully held the gourd to her mouth. She never took her gaze from his face as she drank thirstily.

Fascinated, he watched the water glisten on her full lips. Her long graceful neck arched with every swallow. When she finished, her tongue darted out to capture the last bit of moisture.

Abruptly, she pushed the canteen aside and sat up straighter, glancing around as if she were trying to figure out what had happened.

"They're all dead," he informed her. "I'm sorry if they were kin or friend to you."

"They were devils. I am glad they have gone to meet their God." Her voice was cold, and her words were heavy and hard like stones hurled in anger.

Kade arched his brows in surprise, and then narrowed his eyes in suspicion. This woman was one heck of a puzzlement. She dressed like an Indian, rode with the English, and spoke American better than most people he'd come across. Kade had a feeling, a deep curiosity shadowed this female sure as the night followed day.

He corked the canteen gourd. "Want to tell me your name?" Trying to appear nonthreatening, he leaned back on his elbows and stretched out his legs, crossing them at the ankles.

"Here they call me Blind Deer."

"What do they call you other places?"

"We are not other places." An insolent stare accompanied her words, and by the set of her jaw, he figured it was useless to pursue the issue.

"My name's McCauley. Kade Finnean McCauley." He nodded toward the skittish pinto still running wild. "That's Tucket over there trying to round up your pony. Why did the men you were with want to kill us?" He slipped the vital question in with the mundane in the hope she would be caught unaware and give him a straight answer. He needn't have worried.

"You are free trappers?"

He nodded, staring at her mouth and the healthy color creeping back into her cheeks.

"Then there is your reason why. In this basin you must work for the Company, or you do not work at all."

"Hudson Bay?"

"Yes. I have only been with them a few days. They are less than animals."

"Where were they heading?"

"To their main camp north of here. I was to be a surprise for the man in charge of the Fort. Now he will have an even better surprise when they do not return at all."

The bitterness in Blind Deer's voice disturbed him. She was a might young to speak with a hatred sounding so many years in the making.

"Did they hurt you?" He was almost afraid to hear the answer.

"They beat me once when I tried to run away. But they never touched me otherwise. They told me their leader always got to be first with the women. Then they promised, in great detail, how each would have me later."

Kade sat up, stifling the curse running through his mind. The thought of her being violated by men, who saw her as a commodity to be used and traded, made the gorge rise in his throat.

Out of breath, Tucket returned, interrupting the grisly visions her words had inspired. Gasping for air, the older man leaned over forward, stiff armed, with his hands braced upon his thighs. "I can't catch that spotted critter for love nor money, Kade. He's wilier than a rogue fox."

Blind Deer gave a low whistle. The paint horse came to attention and trotted in their direction, halting a few yards away.

"Well, I'll be switched." Tucket went ramrod straight, then a smile brightened his face. "Do you suppose she could teach me to do such with my mule?"

"No." Blind Deer shook her head. "Mules are stubborn, like people. They do not belong easily, nor answer to another's call."

"She speaks American." Tucket's words rang with surprise.

"That she does, partner."

"Well I'll be. Wasn't expectin' that."

Kade grunted in agreement and gained his feet. "We better get a move on. There could be more unfriendlies around." Figuring to give Blind Deer time to take everything in, he strode toward the enemy's horses, Tucket at his side.

He retrieved the food pouches from the saddlebags and handed them to his partner. "No use letting the perishables go to waste. But we don't have time to tarry. A collective grave is the best we can do for these wretches. And shallow to boot."

"It's poor doin's for sure." Tucket stacked the eatables off to the side under a tree and untied a shovel from one of the horses. "But for likes of these no-accounts, it's better than they deserve."

Kade gathered some stones. "Keep an eye out for the one who rode off. Although, I reckon he's well on his way to report what happened."

****

The burial detail concluded, Tucket moseyed over near the horses to shade up. "What do you want to do about their critters?"

"There's plenty of forage and water right now, but at this elevation they'll have a hard time surviving come winter." Kade glanced over to where Blind Deer sat. "Guess they'll have to come along with us."

"They're right nice animals." Tucket ran one hand down the arched neck of the nearest gelding.

Kade continued to study Blind Deer. "Better than right nice," he mused, before he turned back to face Tucket. "When we get to rendezvous, we turn 'em loose or give 'em away. I won't keep or make a profit from anything that belongs to the Company." His partner nodded and led the animals toward the mules.

Kade retraced his steps and offered the girl a hand-up. She set her jaw, and after two tries, struggled to her feet on her own. He smiled and shook his head. What tribe she came from might be in question, and who her parents were might be a mystery, but white or Indian, she was without a doubt one willful female.

"Pride's an honorable quality, but stubbornness is plain foolish." Not expecting a reply, Kade turned and followed Tucket. Maggie fell in at his side. Mere moments later, he heard Blind Deer fall in several steps behind, her horse trailing along in her wake.

"Looks like she's following us," Tucket observed from the side of his mouth. "What we gonna do with her? Ain't got no place for a woman."

"I know, but same as with the horses, we can't just turn her out."

When they reached the mules, Kade studied Blind Deer. How the heck could two men and a woman as good looking as she was share one small cabin?

Again, refusing his help, she mounted her horse, and although she grimaced, the strong-minded female never uttered a sound. When she shifted her position, her buckskin dress rode up her thighs, revealing long legs—tempting legs—firing his imagination.

He forced his gaze upward to her face. "Do you

want to put in with us?" Part of him wanted her to say yes, but another part knew he was asking for trouble. Big trouble in a little package.

"You saved my life, free trapper. I belong to you now." Her tone—flat and emotionless—made it sound as if she had no choice in the matter and wasn't happy with the idea.

"I also almost killed you," Kade pointed out. "I think that changes any course of action you might feel bound to observe."

She gave him a hint of a smile. Even with streaks of dirt on her face and her hair touseled and matted, her quiet beauty shone through.

"I still choose to go with you, McCauley." Facing straight ahead, she sat her horse tall, her demeanor almost regal, her expression determined.

Figuring that was her final answer and refusing to question why he was so damned pleased with her decision, Kade mounted his mule and turned it toward the trail.

"I hope she can cook," Tucket muttered.

Chapter Three

They rode nonstop for hours. Blind Deer wove her fingers in the mane of her pony, trying to stave off the pain and nausea. Her arm throbbed continually, and now as the sun dipped lower, her resolve faded along with the comforting light.

Although chilled and exhausted, she was grateful to be rid of the English dogs—or had she only traded one keeper for another? The younger of these two strangers had given her free choice to join them—free choice—a precious gift. She in no way felt obliged to travel with these strangers. *She belonged to no man.* But it seemed a better excuse then admitting that living rough these last few weeks had taken an unexpected toll on her body and spirit.

So far, these two men had not mistreated her. But they looked half starved. They were either bad at hunting or had wintered in the high country where food was scarce. Based on the many hides they carried, the latter seemed reasonable. Only strong men survived the winter, and you could never trust a fat mountain man.

She glanced around the gathering gloom. Many things had changed since she lived in the shadow of these mountains. As she traveled with Lord Seton and his brigade, she noticed forts made of logs now stood where before only trees and rock gave testament to life. And there were paths and traces cut into the earth by people and wagons, blotting out the trails worn into existence by the animals roaming wild on the land.

She had been away many years. Was she too late in returning to find her people? What if she had become a dim recollection to those she remembered so vividly? What if they were all dead, wiped out by the invaders to her land or an enemy tribe?

Regardless, better to wander free seeking something which no longer existed, rather than to suffer the certainty of the boarding school and the dirty smoke-filled city.

She would rather die than return to St. Louis.

****

As they wended through the forest, thick and deep, her pony began to lag behind, and the image of the trappers transformed into a soft blur. Blind Deer sighed, letting the old familiar sadness replace her newly acquired concerns.

Her eyesight, poor since birth, had grown no stronger. Thankfully, she could still read and sew, but she could not clearly see all of her surroundings. This was her greatest weakness, and her most highly guarded secret. A secret never to be revealed to her enemies.

Urging her tired pony into a trot, she tried to catch up.

They broke through the trees into a small clearing, the land gently rising to the north. A river curved to the south—the water clear and not too swift. A good place to make camp. Apparently, McCauley thought so too.

"I reckon this will do for tonight," he announced, glancing around.

"Too late to go any farther," Tucket agreed, "especially if we're hopin' to put fresh meat in the pot

26

for supper."

Both men slid from their mules. They hobbled the animals in a grove of lodgepole pine and unloaded the burdens they carried. The snow remained in the shadows offering moisture, and a shimmer of grass promised feed.

Blind Deer dismounted, removed the parfleche bags and bridle from her pony, and turned the little mare loose. In payment for finding trails and speaking to the Crow Indians they had come across, Lord Seton had gifted her with the animal. Over the weeks, she and the pony had grown close. It would not stray from her or the protection of the larger animals.

Lord Seton had been surprised at her choice in horseflesh. The seller warned the animal was foul-tempered and un-ridable, therefore the price was cheap. But she had reassured both men this cayuse pony was the one she wanted. Her people were known for the splendid horses they kept, and for their kinship with them. This animal had obviously been mistreated and misunderstood—an all too familiar feeling. They had an instant connection.

Kade sauntered over, rifle in hand. "Will you be all right on your own while we're off hunting?"

She found irony in his concern. Since leaving the boarding school, she hadn't suffered any true injuries until he'd shot her. Now he seemed to want to protect her. "Yes. I will make a fire in anticipation of your success."

"I don't suppose it would do any good for me to point out you should be resting your arm rather than hauling wood?"

She remained silent.

He gave a snort of amusement. "Didn't think so." Turning, he set off into the woods with the strange dog and Tucket.

Fetching a sturdy rope from her cache of accoutrements, she set out on her own excursion. A tangle of brush and branches downed by winter winds caught her attention. Glad it was not far from camp, she laid a loop of hemp on the ground and then dragged pieces of wood across the rope. Bringing the free ends of rope over the stack and through the loop, she cinched the wood into a tight bundle and hefted it onto her good shoulder.

After unloading the wood at the campsite, she made three more trips. It would be cold here tonight.

Optimistic for their successful hunt, she fashioned a ring of stones, and as her hands recalled the life she once lived, she took flint and steel and created the miracle of a tiny spark. When the char cloth caught, she placed the ember in the tinder bundle, and blew and blew. It burst into flame—always a wonderful surprise, and she gasped in delight and carefully set the fireball atop the pine needles. Soon a hearty blaze devoured the sticks of wood she placed on top.

The sun slipped behind the far ridge, and the clouds in the sky turned pink as summer salmon. But as darkness crept near, the temperature fell. Blind Deer slipped into her woolen capote, threw another log on the fire, and sat listening for the return of the men. She didn't have long to wait. Laughing and joking, Kade and Tucket swaggered back into camp, smiles upon their faces, the game bags laden.

She reached for the catch, but neither man allowed her to help. This seemed odd to her. Cleaning and preparing the meal was women's work, as was hauling water. But they took no notice as they happily performed the chore on the three plump game birds and two rabbits—a feast for so short a time spent hunting.

Never one to sit idle, she went in search of green sticks to use as skewers, and to also gather the wild onions she had seen in the forest while hauling wood.

By the time she returned, the rabbit pelts had been salted, rolled up, and set aside, and Tucket had wrangled a large flat stone into an upright position on the north side of the fire-pit to block the wind and increase the heat. They accepted the sticks she offered, and as they ran the thin ends through the meat, she rubbed the onions on the food. This met with nods of approval.

Then they hunkered down around the circle of stones, and as Mankind had done for one thousand years, they waited for their dinner to cook.

"Nice fire," Tucket put in.

"Couldn't be better," Kade agreed.

Blind Deer did not respond to their compliment. As of late, she had no practice in having her efforts appreciated. She had learned not to care what others thought of her, or at least she had learned not to show it if she did.

"I got a dry needs tending." Tucket got up and rummaged through his belongings. When he sank back down to the ground, he held a little brown jug. Uncorking it, he laid it back upon his bent arm, mountain man style, and raising his elbow directed a good sip into his waiting mouth. His eyes grew wide, and he exhaled as if a fire had been kindled in his stomach.

The jug must contain hard liquor. Her heart raced, and her hand settled over the hilt of her knife. On her few trips to town in St. Louis, she had seen white men ply the local Indians with drink, and she had seen her brothers become children performing antics unbecoming a human being. Many white men also acted the fool under the same circumstances. What would happen here she wondered?

Tucket passed the jug to Kade. After a sampling, the cork went back in place, and both men gave a sigh of contentment and studied the sky.

"Looks to be a clear evening," Tucket commented, "and most likely a cold one."

"Two dog night at least. What a shame we only got Maggie." At the sound of her name, the dog gave a whine and a yawn, and thumped her tail on the ground.

Blind Deer added wood to the fire and snuggled deeper into her blanket coat. She wasn't sure what to make of the dog. When she'd first laid eyes on Maggie, she figured she had died, and the Great Coyote had come to take her to the next realm.

From the stories she'd heard as a child, Coyote had prepared the earth for her people, destroying the monsters and creating the rivers. He also enjoyed playing tricks. Other than having those odd blue eyes, this large dog looked very much like the image she carried in her mind of the sacred beast. The mythical animal was big medicine to her people—for good, as well as in times of trouble. The dog stared at her as if longing to speak while harboring thoughts about her as well. A chill raced through her body.

Finished eating, their spirits restored, drowsy musings quickly followed. Before sleep claimed them completely, they got up to check the animals one more time. Then after a final trip to the woods, they each sought their own space by the fire—curled in their blanket, backs to the wind.

The two men quickly drifted off to sleep, their breathing deep and slow—longrifles at their side. The oblivion Blind Deer sought did not come. The short walk in the woods had revived her senses and set her arm to aching.

She should have cleaned the wound and rinsed out the bandage in the stream. Now it was too dark, and she was too weary, and the fire felt too good. Earlier in the evening she had slipped a handful of club moss and crushed buckhorn leaves under the wrappings to draw out any poison. Good enough until tomorrow.

Squinting up at the night sky, Blind Deer studied the swatch of brightness blurred across the heavens. She saw no twinkling points of light, nor the outline of the animals the elders spoke of in tribal stories. And she saw not the smiling face in Saka'am, the moon. This saddened her most of all, for she loved the moon, a spirit-face filled with the knowledge of many mysteries. Knife in hand, Blind Deer closed her eyes. What must it be like to see such wonders?

****

The next morning, they left the lodgepole pine behind, and relaxed in the saddle, Kade led them down a gentle slope dotted with aspen. Even in the high country, several white-barked trees were already turning. In a few months, when the blaze of orange and gold took hold, the small valley would appear to be on fire.

After several hours, the surrounding area began to

look more familiar to him, and anticipation bolstered Kade's mood. Without prompting, the mules picked up the pace, as if they too sensed they'd soon be within braying distance of the cabin.

Allowing only one respite to relieve themselves and fill their bellies with cold meat and hardtack, the day seemed long. Blind Deer appeared tired, but she never complained—no big surprise there. Trying to read her mood was tougher than tracking a mountain lion on bare rock. But even a painter was more predictable. Was she stubborn, prideful, or foolish? He supposed like everybody else she was a bit of all three, and right now stubborn had the best foothold.

What was she doin' out here on her own anyway? If she stuck around long enough maybe he'd find out—but he wouldn't bet mule and beaver on the outcome.

Besides, more important notions were jumping around in his mind—would they make good time getting to rendezvous, and would they get a fair price for the hides? When you were on your own hook, it could be unreliable doin's. And what about the trade goods from back East? Would they be higher priced than last year, or worse yet, not be there at all?

In '35 whiskey went for three dollars a pint, and beaver three or four dollars a pound. It didn't take a banker to figure the cost of wettin' a dry was becoming astronomical. And then there were the regular supplies they needed—blankets, fish hooks, flour, coffee, and sugar. A new shirt would be nice, especially since he'd cut a chunk out of his present one to fashion a bandage for Blind Deer.

Making a living off the land seemed harder and harder. They'd been fortunate this past season to come across a forgotten valley not yet trapped out. Who could say what next year would bring. The Hudson's Bay Company had expanded their territory to where a family of beaver was hardly left alive to carry on. The only direction left unexplored was Blackfoot land, and folks who ventured there rarely came back.

When they reached a rise, he took a moment and glanced back at the string of animals following in his wake. He grinned at his partner. Tucket sat his horse as if he'd been born there, quite an achievement for an Easterner who once plied his trade as a whaler. The man was like one of them chameleons. He managed to fit in wherever he found himself.

Loose and easy, shoulders slumped, his friend appeared the same as when he sat a chair by the fire. And while he might seem overly comfortable, Kade knew the man's rifle was at the ready and his eyes were always watching for sign—human or critter.

They sure had shared some shinin' times together, and Tucket was as dear to him as ever a father could be. The man knew things about the world that set a body's mind to wondering and puzzling. And he sure made for good company during the winter doldrums.

Kade's gaze slid farther down the line of mules and horses, coming to rest on Blind Deer who insisted on riding at the rear. She ignored him. In fact, she often seemed in a world of her own making—gazing inward rather than out.

She sure was the last thing he'd expected to come across in the middle of a skirmish. Almost like she materialized out of nowhere—like a sprite or a faerie in the stories his Scottish Gran used to tell. Now there were some fanciful thoughts from long ago. Abruptly he turned around and faced forward.

Having Blind Deer around put unexpected ideas in his head, like the uncommon consideration of having a woman to call his own. In the past he'd settled for finding a willing female at rendezvous each year. One who was happy with the foofaraw and trinkets he bought for her. One who would not be insulted when the following winter he'd forget her name and face and remembered only the warmth and the pleasure they'd shared.

What would it be like to have a wintertime love? With a shake of his head, Kade dislodged the outlandish notion and concentrated on the trail, and then a great sadness struck him.

This wild land had come to feel like home, and it might sound foolish, but he believed a body could love a place like a person. After adventuring through these stony mountains for over a decade, the formidable cold peaks and comforting warm valleys were familiar—not always kind, but always there.

Now others came. Some men wanted to own the mountains. There was a heap of difference between kinship and ownership. He gazed up at the jagged white peaks and knew one heartening thing for certain. These monuments, constructed by the hand of God, would be here long after he and Tucket had gone under.

****

When the cabin came into view, Kade's chest tightened, and a joyfulness filled him to overflowing. He reined in his mule and just sat taking in the sight. He hadn't seen their off-season stomping grounds for nearly six months. The windows were still securely shuttered, and the old roof appeared only a little worse for wear for having weathered yet another winter.

"Things look hopeful." Tucket eased his mule up alongside Kade's. "Even the pitch of the porch don't seem much more precarious than I remember."

"Some of the chinking is missing on the windward side."

"That's easy enough to repair. We'll get on it first thing in the morning."

Kade nodded and fell silent. He and Tucket had built this safe-haven. Well, actually, Tucket had done most of the work. Back then, he himself had been a gangly kid with no idea of how to proceed with much of anything, let alone with how to build a cabin. But Tucket had been patient, and they had accomplished the task. And they'd been doing that ever since, the two of them together, accomplishing the task, no matter how difficult.

He wondered if it might be their last year together. Tucket had been making noise about giving up fur trading. Of course, the old man issued the same idle threat every year following the hardships of winter, but he'd sounded serious this time.

Change was in the wind. Right now, it had no name, but it was an unsettling feeling. Just like mountain man luck, there was mountain man intuition, and good or bad, something was comin'.

They rode on to the dwelling, dismounted, and led their animals to the corral. The enclosure was ringed on three sides by sheer rock and closed off on the fourth by several sturdy cut pines run horizontally through the chinked upright posts.

"Make sure them rails be good and secure," Tucket instructed. "Better to spend a minute or two now instead of counting tracks come morning."

Kade smiled and nodded. Tucket was always reminding him to do what he already knew needed doin', but it was good to have someone worry over you—and to have someone to worry over.

He slid the poles into place and lashed them down as Tucket forced open the unwilling cabin door and disappeared inside.

Suddenly, a heap of tangled brush sailed out through the portal. Next came a whoopin' and a hollerin' sound, followed by Tucket, hat in hand, as he gingerly herded along a family of 'possums.

"You ugly little varmints. Step lively, now." His partner followed them as they scurried away. "You're lucky my panniers are full and your hides be too puny to bother with."

Kade let loose with a hearty laugh and went about unloading supplies.

****

Blind Deer stood to one side, waiting for orders as to what to do. When none came, she took it upon herself to once again gather wood. You could never have too much firewood.

As she worked, she watched Tucket and Kade. They went about their chores as if they had shared many seasons together, anticipating one another's moves and needs. Once she had known similar feelings, but now she refused to need anything or anyone. It was safer. No one could control or own you when you held nothing dear.

She also watched the coyote/dog. The way white people treated dogs seemed odd to her. They gave them human names and let them live in the house. They talked to them as friends, yet enslaved them with collars and leashes. Some Indian tribes ate dogs to survive— and some wealthy white women dressed little dogs in clothes and jewels. Again, the two worlds she traveled clashed head on.

Soon a good supply of wood waited outside by the cabin door and inside by the hearth. With the shutters open and opossums gone, their leavings tidied up, the room felt fresh and orderly. There were curtains on the un-glassed windows, clean woolen blankets on the two beds, and a red oilcloth on the lopsided table. How curious that these trappers would bother with such domestic touches. Obviously, this was a home, not just a place to be.

Intending to haul water, she stood in the yard holding two buckets. Kade passed by heading in the other direction, his arms loaded with the last of the goods from the mules.

"There is a creek nearby?"

"Yes. To the west about twenty yards or so. If you wait a minute, I'll go with you."

"Do not concern yourself, McCauley. I will not be in your way or expect you to do woman's work."

Her arm throbbed, but she refused to let it show. If she became a burden, they might turn her out before she recovered enough to endure living on her own again.

"I wasn't worried about your being in the way, Blind Deer. I was worried about you hurting yourself. You sure do take offense at the least provocation."

"I have learned to expect the worst at the least provocation—and I am rarely disappointed."

She followed the route Kade indicated. Why was he being kind to her? Such sentiment did not come without a price, and she wondered what he might want from her. Stumbling over a tree root, she rued her poor vision and hoped he wasn't watching.

McCauley made her worry over useless things like whether or not her face was clean, or if her conversation was pleasing to his ear. She had never felt this way around a man—not with her brothers, or their friends, or the young warrior to whom she was betrothed. Of course, back then she had been very young too, and in love with her pony as she tried hard to be one of the boys.

She quickened her step, seeking the seclusion of the trees up ahead. At the sound of the gurgling stream, she paused and stood motionless. Water was a place where all creatures gathered. Surprising a bear or wolf as they quenched their evening thirst could prove fatal—to surprise a human could be worse. Assured no danger awaited, she continued to the water's edge.

After submerging the buckets to soak and expand the dry wooden slats, she eased down upon a flat rock and loosened the leather pouch from her tack belt. Her precious bundle contained native herbs and white man's medicine. Both held much power, and in the wilderness such knowledge could mean the difference between going on and going under.

With the sleeve of her buckskin dress thrown back over her shoulder, she untied the thong holding the bandage. A sharp pain knifed through her arm. This time she could not stifle her groan.

Scooping up handfuls of freezing cold water, she bathed the shoulder, loosening the last of the stuck-on fabric. Then she rinsed the cloth and allowed it to dry, to be reused another day.

The numbing cold turned to fire as she doused the wound with alcohol from the small vial Sir Reginald had given her for medicinal use during their travels. Lightheaded, she swayed unsteadily and leaned forward, nausea gripping her stomach.

When the sickness passed, she sprinkled powdered willow bark and club moss upon a dry piece of calico stored in her medicine pouch. The flesh continued to burn as she wrapped and tied the bandage into place, and although the wound appeared jagged, the healthy red blood seeping out was a good sign. It should heal fully. One more scar upon her body to rival those etched upon her heart and soul. Reassembling her medicine pouch, she gained her feet.

A branch snapped in the woods. Startled, she turned toward the sound and reached for her knife—the elk-antler hilt biting into her palm.

A blurry figure approached through the gloaming. Too late to run, she unsheathed the Green River blade and stood ready to fight.

The intruder was almost on top of her.

"I came to help fetch back the water." Kade stopped short, warily eying the knife held steadfast between them. "I thought you saw me coming. Otherwise I'd have called out. You were looking right at me."

Your weakness is the weapon of your enemy.

"I was busy tending my wound and did not hear you."

Kade gave her a curious look before retrieving and refilling both buckets with fresh water. Setting one at her feet, he hefted the other, and took off for the cabin. She sheathed her knife, grabbed her medicine bag, and snared the other wooden handle.

She wished to speak, but what would be of interest to this man? Nothing came to mind, so they walked in silence. Blind Deer had never found quietude so disturbing. Oddly, while the silence seemed troubling, Kade's nearness felt reassuring.

Lengthening her stride to match his, she risked a sideways glance his way. He walked tall and proud, yet with an easy gait, and his long brown hair, tied back with a thong, showed red streaks of fire whenever it was struck by the sun's rays. His beard, worn short, was of a darker hue.

Catching her staring at him, Kade smiled. The action reached all the way to his eyes, kindling a spark in the rich dark-blue color.

She quickly glanced away, refusing to look again until they reached the cabin.

Without thinking, she began to prepare supper, boiling the potatoes stored at the cabin, and panfrying the duck Tucket had shot. This time her efforts met with no resistance. Right up until the last glimmer of daylight, the men worked at repairing a corner of the roof, and at patching the hole in the wall where the possums had gained entrance. Now they both seemed done in.

At a rustling noise Blind Deer peeked over her shoulder. The older trapper rummaged about in a trunk wedged between the two beds. A heartbeat later she jumped as a screeching sound filled the air. After adjusting the fiddle with great care, Kade's partner managed to coax a less excruciating sound from the instrument.

Kade lit a candle lantern, and Tucket ran through

his repertoire, and she could not help but enjoy the musical interlude.

Sitting by the door, Kade tipped his chair back against the wall, then he reached down to scratch the big dog lying at his side. "Where do you hale from, Blind Deer?"

Coming at her out of the blue, the question took her by surprise. The Bitterroot Valley had been her home, but she had yet to make it back there in her current travels. Besides, why should he care?

"Where I am from depends upon whom you ask." At her evasive answer, Kade raised a brow. Regretting her sharp words, she continued. "Having a white mother and an Indian father, the Salish say I am from the circle that overlaps. They think I am honored to walk in two worlds. The Missionaries say I belong nowhere, and I corrupt both worlds."

"And what do you say?"

She hesitated, mulling over her answer. Here was a question no one had bothered to ask her before. "I am just me. And for now, I am where I belong."

"Or maybe you're a world unto yourself." Kade tipped his chair forward, and the front legs thumped back down onto the floor.

Did he laugh at her? His expression was serious, and kindness lived in his eyes.

Kade McCauley was vastly different from most dogface white men she'd met.

****

Kade decided not to ask any more questions, and when supper ended, he helped Blind Deer clean up the dishes and utensils. As she banked the coals in the fireplace, he followed her movements with what he hoped was an unobtrusive gaze. He couldn't help but be transfixed at seeing a woman in their little cabin tending to such chores.

"You can have my bed," he offered when she returned from visiting the trees.

"Or mine," Tucket quickly put in.

"I will be fine by the hearth." Mouth set in a firm line, she sat down to take off her moccasins.

Kade opened his mouth, not to argue, as he knew that would be for naught, but to warn her. Maggie usually slept in that spot. Before he could utter a word, she held up her hand indicating there was to be no further discussion. He took the hint, curious as to how this was about to play out.

Blind Deer diligently made a nest with the hides and blankets he'd offered her, and when everyone seemed settle in for the night Kade blew out the candle lantern. A few moments later, Maggie padded across the room, her toenails clicking on the floorboards as she headed for her usual place to bed down. Discovering the space occupied, the dog let out a menacing snarl.

Unable to suppress a smile, Kade waited in the dark for Blind Deer to call for help, or for her to come running to his side.

Instead he heard an even more ominous growl as Blind Deer defended her territory. That gal had a mind of her own, and the plumb crazy courage to back it up. With a whine, one exceptionally pitiful, Maggie turned tail and moved to a new spot—farther from the hearth, and closer to the foot of Kade's bed.

Chapter Four

Glancing out the cabin window, Blind Deer watched Kade and Tucket as they tended to the morning chores.

These men were curious to her. Neither had tried to sneak into her bed, and although they treated her like a sister, she would continue to sleep with knife-in-hand. To be honest, the men did not truly scare her, but how readily she had become accustomed to the arrangement of traveling with them frightened her a great deal.

Grabbing the bucket holding the breakfast wash water, she stepped to the door and heaved the contents into the yard. Her injured arm gave a hearty twinge, but it was bearable. The wound was much better today, and soon she could leave and fend for herself if she had to. But this was the safest she felt in a long while. And certainly, the safest since parting company with Lord Seton. What could it hurt to stay a while longer?

Refilling the bucket at the stream, she returned to the cabin and softly closed the door. If she stayed, she must not be lulled into false contentment. Nothing had changed. These two meant nothing to her. She must take advantage of their sympathy and kindness, using whatever it took to keep going, to keep searching for her tribe.

She hadn't always felt this way. Once she had trusted to the future, and to the magic of love and hope.

But if measured by grief endured, that was long ago. Now she believed only in herself. To find her Salishan people was the reason for which she lived, and although many years had passed since she'd seen the Bitterroot Valley, she spent a lot of time there in her mind.

The cabin door flew open. Blind Deer jumped and turned toward the noise. Favoring his right foot, Kade lumbered forward and flung himself toward the nearest chair.

"Dang mule." He bent forward to unlace his moccasin. "Stepped on my foot—not once but twice."

"Let me help." She crouched at his side. "Does the animal seek to harm you on purpose?" She slid the leather from his foot.

"No. It was my fault for getting between the two of them hitched to a rail."

"Then I suppose shooting and eating this animal is out of the question." She peered up at him through her lashes.

He chuckled and relaxed back in the chair. "Sorry for bursting in on you in such a lather."

Rolling one of the stumps used for sitting near the hearth closer to Kade, she up-ended it, placed a folded blanket on top, and rested his foot upon the woolen cushion. "I just brought in fresh water from the stream. The cold will help your pain and discourage the swelling." Soaking a cloth in the icy water, she applied it to the top of his foot. While holding the cloth in place, she noticed a scar near the bruised flesh. Red and twisted, the old wound curved upward, disappearing beneath the leg of Kade's buckskin pants. The healed scar still appeared angry, as if refusing to be forgotten. "Did the mule do this too?" Gently, she ran a finger across the puckered flesh.

"No." Kade shook his head. "An Indian brave accommodated me there. After he killed my parents and grandmother."

Blind Deer drew back her hand as if touching fire. "You must hate Indians." She leaned away from him.

"Just that one."

"But not all?"

"Why should I? They haven't all tried to kill me. At least not yet. Although the Blackfoot tribe does have a long-standing hate for white folk. Since Lewis and Clark came through, many a trapper's gone under crossing paths with a Blackfoot. But no, I don't hate all Indians—or even most."

She had a hard time not despising all white people. And even if he did not, she hated the entire Blackfoot nation. They were forever enemies of her people, always were, always would be.

"They took from you what can never be replaced."

"They didn't—he did. There's a difference. Besides, it was a long time ago, and I don't have the desire or the wherewithal to persecute an entire group of people. I've been too busy just trying to stay alive out here."

"How is it you were not killed as well?"

"It wasn't for lack of tryin' on his part." Kade's expression turned thoughtful. "It was springtime, and we'd just moved to Missouri. I was ten years old, and that morning playing down by the creek in the hopes of catching a few bullfrogs. Then I heard a ruckus going on up by the house. When I got there my parents and Gran were dead, and the biggest meanest-looking Indian I'd ever dreamed in a nightmare started coming after me. I stood frozen with fright. He grabbed me by one ankle and held me upside down, shaking me like a big dog with a little rabbit.

"The eagle claw hanging from a strap on his wrist dug into my leg, and the pain brought me to my senses. I twisted and kicked, and broke loose of his grasp, but as I dropped toward the ground, he tried to regain his grip, and the talon gouged a great bloody tear down and around my leg."

"You were very brave."

"I was lucky. I hit the dirt running, never knowing how bad I was hurt. In about ten yards I smacked headfirst into Tucket. He shot that Indian dead in his tracks, and then sewed me up. That's how we met, Tucket and me. He knew my pa from when we lived back East, and as if sent by God to be my guardian angel, he'd come to visit that particular day on his way through to the Stony Mountains."

She studied the scar anew.

"Now don't you go criticizing Tucket's handiwork." Kade tried to lighten the mood. "It ain't pretty, but as far as I'm concerned it's fancier than any stitching ever graced a rich lady's under-pinnings. Besides, I was jumpin' around quite a bit while he was sewing."

Blind Deer smiled. "And how is it you know so much about rich ladies underclothing?"

"We get to town on occasion."

An unexpected moment of regret flashed through her. He'd shown no interest in seeing her unmentionables. "It was good of Tucket to take you in."

"That's what it's all about, Blind Deer. Folks helping folks."

More white man ideas. She straightened and turned away, tearing another cloth into long wide strips. Kade and Tucket had taken her in, but as of yet, she felt no gratitude or debt to them. She did not know if she would have done the same for them.

Retrieving her bag of medicines now residing near her sleeping pallet, she selected a small jar of salve and rubbed the earthy smelling cream on his foot where it was already showing shades of purple and red.

"What's that stuff?" Kade's nose wrinkled.

"Bear root, cobwebs, and wild mint leaves. It tastes even worse than it smells. Be glad it is for your bruises and not for a pain in your stomach." Following the application of balm, she wrapped the strips of fabric around and around, starting at his toes and ending just above his ankle bone.

"Well it sure feels better already. Thank you, Blind Deer. I'm much obliged to you for your help."

"You are welcome, McCauley." She still couldn't bring herself to use his Christian name. "You should soak it in the cold stream later."

"I will, and I reckon it'll be good as new in a few days. At least I hope so. We'll be leaving once we catch our breath and finish making repairs on our traps and paraphernalia. We can't afford for anything to go wrong between now and when we get to rendezvous."

"There will be Indians there?" She felt his gaze upon her as she busied herself putting away the ointment.

"Yes. There usually are. Quite a few."

"From all tribes?"

"Again, yes. And plenty of foofaraw and gewgaws a young gal such as yourself might be interested in."

"I seek only my people." Inwardly Blind Deer smiled. Did Kade try to tempt her to join them with the promise of blankets, beads, and cooking pots? "Where is this gathering to take place?" Before parting company with Lord Seton at Fort Hall, she had heard talk about the location, but she wanted details.

"It's on the Green again this year, the Siskeedee-Agie, where it meets Horse Creek. I sure hope things go better there than they did back in '33." He gave a shudder. "That was cold doin's, what with the unexpected icy weather coming on like some bad omen. Then a crazed wolf kept hanging around the camp. The critter bit twelve men. But after they shot that pitiful beast, a snow eater blew through camp, and the weather remained warm from there on out. One thing for sure, a body never knows what to expect at rendezvous."

"I have heard of animals losing their senses and biting humans."

"There's no need for concern," he reassured. "In all the years Tucket and I have been going, I only heard of that occurring once. Mostly there's just high spirited fun and tangle-foot induced chicanery. Of course, according to Tucket, there are plenty of other strange happenings in the world."

"Like what? Strange is not usually good."

"It can be. Did you see it rain fire that same year? I'll never forget it. Stars were a shootin' across the sky one after another. It seemed like the end of creation, or maybe what it must have been like at the beginning.

"Some while later, we met a fellow from London, England, and he called it a meteor shower. Sure was rainin' stars that night. Ain't seen nothing like it since."

"I do remember." Blind Deer nodded, fighting to

48

keep the sadness from her voice. Her poor vision had prevented her from witnessing what everyone else had enjoyed with awe and wonderment. No one at the orphanage recalled ever seeing such an event. One girl called it watching the stars dance. At such a beautiful thought, Blind Deer had cried, her tears blurring her vision even more.

Tucket came to the door and poked his head in, and her sad thoughts scattered. "How's the foot? You been gone so long I thought ya went under." Not waiting for an answer, he ambled forward, grabbed a hunk of Kade's buckskins just above the ankle and raised the injured leg to facilitate a closer inspection of the foot in question.

"Looks all right to me." He dropped Kade's foot only half-gently back upon the folded blanket. "What you doin' palaverin' when there's still plenty of work to do. I knowed a man with only one foot could run circles around you. Why you young beaver don't know what hard work is." With a shake of his head, he turned and headed back to the corral.

"I'm comin' old man. Don't get your boudins in a twist." Kade replaced his rather bedraggled moccasin, gained his feet, and made for the door. "Heat must be getting to him. It's quite a bit warmer down here than in the high mountains." He paused and glanced back at her. "Thank you again for doctorin' me up."

She watched him walk away, his gait fairly even.

When he caught up to Tucket, the old man slapped Kade on the back and pointed to a jumble of traps waiting to be cleaned and repaired. "You bein' so incapacitated, you can work on those while sittin' on your backside."

"But you declared, quite loudly as I recall, you were quitting the beaver business. Won't be needing no traps." Kade sounded smug like he'd caught Tucket in a trap of his own words.

"Ones in working condition sell better. Get on it."

Blind Deer didn't mean to, didn't want to, but she smiled, enjoying their antics.

Chapter Five

Standing in the dusty parade arena, Captain Stuart Sulgrave studied his Hudson's Bay brigade of misfits. The summer had turned unusually hot, and the heat from the relentless sun fueled his anger to near the boiling point—making him almost yearn for the mind-numbing cold of winter.

Three of his men had been killed, and Carson, the one who made it back alive, was wounded and kept jabbering on about some female Indian with green eyes, and two trappers who fought with the strength of four men. No doubt more backwoods nonsense, so typical of the rabble he was obliged to command.

His men should have killed the free trappers, and appropriated the woman, the furs, and the supplies. But accomplishing such a mission would have entailed these half-wits executing a comprehensive plan of action without direct orders.

Repeatedly slapping his riding crop against his thigh, he paced to and fro, his steps marking time with the whip-like sound. Damn them all to hell and back. He directed his ire indiscriminately at the dead men as well as at the men who'd killed them.

"You two." With his short whip, he pointed out the men he'd chosen. "You're to leave immediately." He hated wasting manpower on these interlopers. He would need as many men as possible when they reached the horrendously vulgar confluence of mankind called rendezvous.

"Find the free trappers and bring them to me."

The two men he'd selected swallowed hard and stared straight ahead. He could almost smell their fear.

"Carson is well enough to give you directions as to where the skirmish took place, and you can take a couple Bug's Boys. Make sure it's the two Blackfoot who have been causing trouble in the Fort. Might as well put them to work tracking—it's about all they're good for. When you complete your mission, return here. If you're gone longer than one week, we'll already be heading south. I trust you have the brains to find the location of the gathering. Don't come back without the murdering rabble you're hunting, or a good accounting of how they met their demise.

"Dismiss the men—" He nodded to his second in command. "—and carry on."

The two men selected went to saddle their horses and draw supplies.

What a sorry bunch—the whole lot of them. Sulgrave showed no compassion for the living or dead and didn't care who knew. Controlling Fort Elise, a desolate outpost of the Hudson's Bay Company, didn't leave room for such an emotion. It didn't leave room for much of anything except dreams for the future, and a well-thought-out plan of escape.

He took to the ramparts and watched the two men and their Indian guides disappear into the shimmering heat. There was change in the air. He'd heard rumors the American Fur Trade Company was on the verge of collapse, and the demand for beaver back East was dwindling. Soon these annual rendezvous of trappers, traders, and Indians would be a thing of the past, and God only knew where he might be sent next. Good thing his plans didn't include being on this continent come 1837.

His assignment at Fort Elise could only be interpreted as a personal affront, more a prison sentence than a command. He hated this uncivilized land and being so far away from England ate at his soul. Now, because returning home was out of the question, moving on was the only answer.

Prior rumors about his liaison with a female French spy had ruined his service to the King within the upper echelons. The rumors were true, of course, but on his part, it had been merely a case of lust, not espionage. Not so for his paramour. Too bad she'd been caught and hanged. Barely escaping the same fate, the result had been his banishment to this godforsaken place. Still he commanded men and ruled his own little empire. No one told him what to do or when to do it. No one except George Simpson.

When the Hudson's Bay Company merged with the Northwest Company in '21, George Simpson had been appointed governor of the northern department—a position upon which Sulgrave had once set his own sights. Another slap in the face.

Being a stubborn Scotsman, Simpson refused to retire or die. The insufferable old man was unpredictable and drunk with his own sense of power. And he had a habit of making unannounced inspections, wearing his damnable long black coat and top hat, bagpipers announcing his arrival with that earsplitting screeching they called music.

But Simpson was in for a big surprise. Altering the

HBC books and appropriating money by selling undeclared hides, Sulgrave finally had enough money to retire in style to a home he owned free and clear. For the past several years, the money he'd been pilfering had been sent to a friend in Broc, Switzerland. Now he was a silent partner in a sheep ranch, and he intended to make a killing in the wool market, which was booming due to industrialization.

He'd visited the area back then with his former French lover, declaring it the perfect place to live in comfort and anonymity. How could one not like a country that gave the world chocolate, absinthe, cheese, and a decent timepiece? Not to mention beautiful women to cater to his needs. And as an added bonus, it felt as if he were stealing directly from Simpson—making the endeavor all the sweeter and worth the risk.

Returning to his quarters, he closed the door and lit a cigar, or a close facsimile. An old rope burning would have smelled less foul, but again, it was better than nothing. Nothing. That's what there was plenty of out here. Setting the smoldering stub aside, he grabbed a bottle of brandy. The liquid lightning washed down his throat and set his stomach on fire as he continued to contemplate his future.

Touching up the wax on his mustache and oiling his hair, he checked his reflection in the mirror. No need to resemble a philistine even though forced to live like one.

He'd withstood nearly five years in this uncouth no-man's land, and this was his last chance at the life he deserved. To lose it now would be unbearable. This fear of failure drove him. He refused to be bested by anyone. On so many levels, survival always boiled down to kill or be killed. Sometimes the killing was necessary, sometimes just for fun.

He headed for the stables.

"Lieutenant—ready my mount." A good hard ride would take his mind off things.

Once in the saddle, he rode as if in pursuit of glory—or as if something terrible followed close behind. He heard the man at the gate choking and coughing in the cloud of dust churned up in his wake.

Chapter Six

The next morning, although wide awake, Kade remained motionless. Tucket had risen earlier and gone outside, and from his bed Kade watched Blind Deer as she busied herself fanning last night's embers into flames.

He enjoyed watching her in the mornings as she purposefully went about the small cabin, quiet as a church mouse. The only sound came from the gentle tapping together of shells and tin cones decorating her buckskin dress. A muted tapping he didn't always hear during a busy day.

The fire caught and took hold, crackling cheerfully in the old stone fireplace, and the heat brought a glow to Blind Deer's cheeks. Sitting near the hearth, with those sweet lips pursed, she gathered her hair into a long thick braid, tying it off with a strip of leather decorated with porcupine quills. How much longer could he go without tasting such a kissable mouth?

She rose and reached for the dumpling dust, and he hoped she intended to make a batch of flapjacks. His stomach growled at the idea. She had the knack for creating this savory treat by adding prepared herbs and greens she found in the forest. This had become his favorite breakfast.

"Get back, dog."

She never called the animal by name, always just

dog, as if refusing to become too familiar with Maggie, or for that matter, with any of them. Kade smiled, remembering the first night they had spent together in the cabin and the fight between Maggie and Blind Deer for territorial rights. A truce of some sort had been declared as now the two of them got along tolerably well.

He tried but couldn't stifle a yawn.

"Good morning, sleepy one." Not turning around, she spoke softly while stirring batter in the bowl. "You rise later every day. By next snow fall you will be getting up just in time to see the sun set."

Although he couldn't see if a smile curved her lips, he recognized her humor. "Will you still make me flapjacks, even if it's for supper instead of breakfast?"

She turned to face him, her expression wistful—the mirth had slipped away. "I doubt I will be here come winter."

They studied one another, and the rush of emotion when their gazes met seemed to catch fire, creating an almost tangible heat. Then the feeling dissolved away before being allowed to take hold, and the fragileness of the tie between them came glaringly to the surface.

Blind Deer turned away, her shoulders stiff as if in determination, and with her back straight as a lodgepole, she concentrated on her cooking. Kade silently got up and dressed.

At times he wished Blind Deer would stay forever. But as far as he could figure, they were both wandering-spirit types, and the chance of them meandering in the same direction for long seemed unlikely.

In the past few days, the only thing he'd learned

about her was she liked a good pipe of kinnikinick after her evening meal, and at daybreak, she chanted an odd combination of Indian words and American poetry. It was mighty slim knowledge upon which to base any hopes of a relationship, granted the time they'd spent together didn't amount to a poke of jerky in the true scheme of things,

Yawning in earnest, he ran his hands through his hair and sat down on a three-legged stool by the front window. "Tucket still out talking to the trees?"

"He was." Blind Deer reached for Kade's dry moccasins where they hung on a peg by the hearth, then handed him the footwear. "He is out seeing after the mules now."

Their fingertips touched, and Kade glance up—lost in those clear green eyes of hers. He felt as if Blind Deer could see right down deep inside him. Did she recognize the wanting and desire waiting for her there?

Reading Blind Deer's thoughts was darn near impossible. With the other females he'd come across, he'd had no trouble interpreting their needs. He didn't always understand the why element of what they wanted, but there was usually no mistaking the what part. This gal was definitely different. How long had it taken her to learn to hide herself so successfully? Sad to think what had driven her to do so.

Finished lacing his moccasins, being careful of his still tender right foot, he straightened and shifted his gaze to stare out the window. He should get a move on, but captivated by sharing this time with Blind Deer he remained seated, enjoying the moment.

Just being near her gave him a sense of joy, like when he came upon a doe in the forest, or a waterfall, or an eagle soaring as high as the mountains. The wonder of her gripped him hard and deep.

"Eat while the food is still hot," she coaxed, handing Kade a plate of flapjacks and some refried duck.

The sound of her voice broke the spell he'd fallen under. Taking the offering, he sat at the little table. She took to the chair across from him, and for a moment they both silently did their share of eating. It tasted even better than he'd imagined.

"Thank you for cooking breakfast near every morning. And good ones they are at that."

"You are welcome. I am thankful for your shelter and protection."

She seemed relaxed, and a bit talkative, so he jumped at the chance to continue the conversation. "We'll be leaving in two days. Have you decided if you want to go with us?"

"No."

"No, you haven't decided, or no you don't want to go? You should join us." He was disappointed she seemed so willing to leave him and Tucket. "We sure have enjoyed your company and nurturing ways. The cabin never seemed more like a home." The last few words he'd intended to think not speak, but they were out there now and there was no taking them back. "You shouldn't miss the rendezvous." He kept talking, trying to make light of what he'd blurted out.

"Someone at the great council might know the whereabouts of my tribe?"

"Sure, I bet they might." He had no idea really, but anything was possible. Several different tribes usually showed up, and he couldn't help using every enticement available to get her to come along.

"Then yes, I will go with you. My tribe no longer makes camp at the place I remembered. I must search for them elsewhere." Now she only picked at her food, and her sadness seemed to hang in the air around them.

"Is that what you were doing when we came across you—searching for your people?

"Again, yes. At first, I traveled with a group. Their leader, Sir Reginald, was determined to help me even after we found my family's winter camp deserted. We headed farther west, making it all the way to Fort Hall, where we stopped for supplies. Three days travel from there, he was laid low, sick with fever, a recurring illness from his military days. Using herbs and powders from my medicine bag, we got him well enough to make it back to the Fort. The men there spoke of the rendezvous. I believe Lord Seton wanted to go there too."

"Then there's another reason you should come with us. Is he doing better?"

"I do not know. Unlikely to be up and about soon, and knowing I left him in good hands, we parted company—regardless of his warning about traveling alone. But rather than go to the Bitterroot Valley, I turned back to the east, the way we had come, hoping to find this gathering of which all of you speak."

"All alone? Out here?"

"It seemed like a good idea at the time. But Sir Reginald's protests soon proved well founded, and I realized the true danger and foolishness of my decision when the English devils captured me."

She sounded defensive, but the words Kade bit back were of surprise, not admonishment. Heaven above, she was an independent creature. Most men wouldn't come this far west alone. Despite her poor judgment he had to admire her courage and tenacity.

"So, what was at the camp you came across before this Lord fellow took sick?

"Nothing good. Only bits of trade cloth and rotted leather, and tipi rings surrounded by scorched earth and bones. The place I once knew was gone except for the memories. That is why I must keep searching elsewhere."

"I'm sorry. Maybe Tucket and I can help you after we do our trading."

She gave a slight smile and rose to put food on a third plate. Sunlight filtered in around her, adding a sparkle to the dust motes swirling in the air by the hearth. The halo of light surrounding her prompted fanciful thoughts. Maybe Blind Deer was some kind of Indian princess.

A fun notion to consider, but in his heart he knew such ideas, like his finding a wintertime love, were wishful thinking, and that never got him anywhere except behind in his chores.

"After rendezvous, you could partner up with us."

"Finding my people is all I care about. Nothing else matters." Her sharp words took him by surprise, along with her dead serious expression. Was she trying to say she had no place for him or anybody else in her life?

Figuring more talk would do no good and lead to frustration, Kade gulped down the last of his food. "I better go help Tucket."

He set his tin plate near the hearth and grabbed the one Blind Deer made up for the older man. "Thank you again for breakfast. I'll deliver this for you."

Fearing she might change her mind about going with them, he left the cabin quickly before another word could be spoken by either one of them. At least she would be with them for a few more weeks, even though with her own purpose in mind, and not because she sought his company.

He lost no time heading for the sanctity of the corral and Tucket's familiar face, but after several steps, he slowed his pace to ease his injured foot. His conversation with Blind Deer left him unsettled. On the one hand he felt glad she was coming, on the other downhearted knowing she'd eventually seek a path bound to take her far away from him. Disappointment had him scowling at the realization.

"Here's your breakfast." His thoughts far away, he handed off the food to Tucket. "How are the mules?"

"They look better than you." Tucket gave Kade the once over. "You off your feed or somethin'?"

"Somethin'." Kade glanced back at the cabin.

It didn't take his friend long to figure out the cause of his distress.

"She sure be a comely addition to the cabin." Tucket nodded with a sideways glance at Kade. "Cooks good too. I was afraid she'd be feedin' us nothing but Mandan stew or succotash, but other than these here flapjacks, she ain't cooked the same thing twice since we've been here."

"I asked her to go with us to rendezvous. That okay with you?" Kade supposed he should have checked with Tucket before making the offer.

"Sure, Kade. It'll save me the torture of havin' only your face to look at all the way there."

Even his partner's playful jibe didn't shake Kade from his thoughts. Rather than retaliating with a remark of his own, he wandered over to the heap of firewood needing to be split. Balancing a large piece of aspen on the chopping stump, he swung the big axe up and over his head. The downward blow seemed to shake the surrounding earth.

He guessed it was just not meant to be. But then why had his path crossed Blind Deer's with such fire and wonderment only to strike off in another direction so quickly? Thinking of her being gone made him feel lonely, not a doin' which often plagued him. And he already had enough on his mind.

So many things in life depended on timing—and mountain man luck. Even reaching the site in the valley of the Green took proper planning. If they left too early, they might be caught in a late spring storm. If they tarried, they would miss the opening days of trading. Late-comers couldn't bargain, they took whatever they could get, and he and Tucket had worked too hard for these hides not to get the best price.

Then there were the supply wagons from back East. They would take the familiar route up the North Platte, thence up the Sweetwater and over South Pass. They traveled on luck, too, as well as on knowhow. And even with Fitzpatrick and Sublette's experience, and Moses "Black" Harris leading them, who knew if they would make it there? Between bad weather, accidents, and hostiles, there was great potential for trouble betwixt the Missouri and the rendezvous site.

****

Kade kept at the backbreaking work for over an hour.

Tucket continued to examine the mules, picking hooves, and checking eyes for signs of problems, and ears for signs of ticks. Then he inspected their tack and gear.

By mid-morning there was enough wood chopped to keep a fort-full of soldiers warm for an entire winter. Finally, ready for a break, Kade stood amid the splintered mound of aspen.

As he wiped the sweat from his face with the sleeve of his shirt, he noticed Blind Deer heading into the woods, a basket in her arms. What did she go to gather? Probably still too early for any berries to be ripe up here. Unable to resist, he abandoned the axe and headed in the same direction.

Carefully picking her way over the uneven footing, she seemed to find the easiest course through the trees and rocky terrain. Reaching a large cottonwood, she stopped to gather moss from the north side. So, this was the purpose of her excursion. Sheet after sheet, she carefully chose then placed each piece in the bottom of the basket. She did not take all from any one tree, and she did not take any from some. Like a curious sparrow, she scrutinized every trunk before beginning her harvest.

Moseying along, she talked and clucked to the birds, rabbits, and squirrels. They did not scurry from her path as they did from his—they more or less made way for her passage. When it seemed she had a goodly supply of the moss, Blind Deer turned her attention to picking other plants, ones Kade would have dismissed as weeds. She chose and gathered them with the same thoughtfulness and care assuring him they were of a more worthy nature.

It didn't appear she was going to wander much farther, and feeling guilty for secretly watching her, he decided to return to the cabin. She should be safe enough, and Maggie would warn him if anything was amiss.

Just as he turned to leave, Blind Deer set her basket aside and stretched out on a hillside of grass dotted with the first meadow flowers. The sunlight trimmed everything in gold, and he soaked in each detail, making sure the image would never fade. Next season when the wind howled and the snow blew fierce, this remembrance would warm his heart.

He longed to lie beside her, just to talk or share the silence, but he couldn't bring himself to intrude upon her solitude. If she had wanted his company, she would have asked. After watching a few moments longer, he slipped away.

As he finished stacking the wood he'd split, Blind Deer returned. She took the basket into the cabin and came back with a tin cup of fresh water. "I see you have been working very hard today." She offered him the drink, making sure not to stand too closely.

"It's good for the soul." A lie of course, as his soul felt anything but good. In fact, it felt troubled as it never had before. He took the water from her, drinking non-stop, not even pausing for a breath.

"How's the arm healing?" He set the cup down on an upturned barrel and tried to think of something more to say to keep her at his side.

"Soon it will be as it once was. There is no permanent injury."

"I'm sure glad to hear that. You know it was an accident, right? I would never hurt you on purpose."

"I believe you, McCauley."

He took a step closer. When she didn't tense up or shy away, he reached out and touched the flower tucked behind her left ear. She smelled fresh and spicy, like a sage prairie in early fall.

Emboldened, he slid his fingers from the flower to her hair, daring to touch the thick braid looped over her shoulder. She smiled at him, tentatively, sweetly, and a wave of longing flashed through him, almost bringing him to his knees. She seemed unaware of the effect she had upon him.

When he lowered his arm to his side, she retrieved the blossom, cradling it in her hand. "I should not have picked it. Now it will die all the sooner for having served my vanity."

"Maybe it rejoices," Kade countered, "finding the sacrifice of little consequence. Maybe it feels even more special because you chose it above all the other flowers covering the hillside."

"How did you know I found it on the hill?" Her demeanor swiftly changed, but she didn't take a step backward.

"Now don't get riled." He placed what he hoped was a reassuring hand on her shoulder. "I saw you leaving, and I didn't know how far you were going. I was worried about you. I only followed at a distance, and only watched you for a short while."

"You were worried about my welfare?"

Kade nodded. She seemed to believe him but not understand why.

"Thank you for not intruding." Her smile returned. "It was a peaceful moment—without fear. It has been a long time since I felt one with the land." The shoulder he touched relaxed. The soft buckskin beneath his fingers still held the warmth of the sun.

Could they be more different from one another? Blind Deer came from two worlds, and his seemed different from both of hers. Lately, there appeared to be an overabundance of worlds, the people in them ready to war with one another at the least incentive.

Everything was getting too complicated.

He leaned forward intent on kissing those lips he'd been dreaming about—there was nothing complicated about that. She placed both hands on his chest as if to hold him back. His enthusiasm plummeted. Then she slipped her arms around his neck, as if seeking more to be held rather than kissed.

Beneath the soft buckskin dress, Blind Deer's unbound breasts pressed flat against his chest, firing hot emotions. This time the heat did not come from the sun. He wanted to pick her up, carry her to the cabin, and make love to her. Knowing such a move would be unseemly of him, and frightening to her, he overcame the pounding urgency.

Yet unwilling to let her go without a little taste, he drew back slightly and kissed her, short and feather-light. "I've wanted to do that for an awfully long time."

"It is good you are of a persistent nature, McCauley."

Their lips met again, this time longer, harder, more ardently. When her closeness became too big of a temptation, urging him to take more than he felt she would be willing to give, he eased her away, slowly removing her arms from around his neck. Her shy smile indicated he'd done the right thing. Side by side, shoulder to shoulder, they walked back to the cabin—if not as true friends, at least as companions—this in itself marked a big step in their relationship.

Too bad once they arrived at rendezvous, he would lose her forever.

****

The next few days scurried by like rabbits on the run.

McCauley didn't kiss her again, but the closeness she felt, and the occasional touching of hands as they went about their daily lives was a gift. These special moments reclaimed once lost memories of contentment and hope—feelings she missed and wanted to know again. She felt whole rather than made up of two pieces held together by determination and circumstance. But McCauley was a distraction and finding her family or what had become of them had to come first.

****

The day of their departure broke gently and sunny, so the feeling of sorrow in leaving the little cabin came as a surprise to Blind Deer. Twisting around, she glanced back at the weathered structure and listing porch. The windows were shuttered, and no smoke drifted from the crooked chimney. The cabin seemed sad too.

She watched and watched, until the view became a blur. She would remember it like that—soft and welcoming, no harsh details or imperfections to mar her memory of the days spent there with McCauley. Facing forward, she decided sometimes bad vision took the sharp edges off the world, making it a place of comfort rather than a place of struggle.

After several miles, Kade slowed their pace, and a feeling of unrest overtook her emotions, but glancing from side to side, she saw no sign of man nor beast. Traveling now in their new order, insisted upon by the men, Tucket brought up the rear of their caravan. He kept at the same easy pace but sat more erect.

Snorting and balking, Kade's mule abruptly halted, the whites of its eyes flashing.

Tucket rode up alongside of her and handed off the leads of the pack mules and horses, then he headed for Kade.

Maggie barked, her hackles raised.

"What the devil's got into these critters?" Tucket reined in next to Kade.

"Darned if I know. I don't see one thing out of the ordinary. Haven't crossed any tracks or sign.

"I don't smell nothin'." Tucket put his nose to the wind and gave another few good sniffs.

Kade dismounted and unsheathed his Kentucky longrifle from its beaded buckskin case. "Stay here with Blind Deer and keep your eyes open." He glanced around, his free hand on the Charleville pistol hooked to his belt. "Could be more Hudson's Bay boys about in these parts. I'll walk on up ahead and reconnoiter a bit. Better keep Maggie back too." Armed with the firearms and knife, Kade silently picked a path through the tall grass.

Then he was gone. Disappeared. Swallowed up by the earth.

Blind Deer urged her horse forward.

"You stay put." Tucket's quick forceful command cut her efforts short. "And mind the animals." His dark expression added the unspoken *don't argue*.

As she worked to control the horses and pack animals, Tucket dismounted and eased forward.

Whining, Maggie followed at his heels.

"Please, let him be all right. Smile your protection down upon him." In desperation, she directed her whispered plea to the Great Spirit of her childhood, as well as the white God her mother believed in.

Chapter Seven

Kade couldn't move. He rested flat on his stomach, head to one side, dirt packed around his body. It felt like half a mountain was heaped on his backside. At least he could breathe—barely. The hood of his woolen capote had flopped forward over his face, keeping all but a sprinkling of the dirt from entering his mouth and nose.

What in hellfire had happened?

His right hand grasped what felt like a rotting hide, and the ferocious smell surrounding him did not encourage him to take a deep breath—even if he could. He moved his left leg—a large stone bit into his anklebone. Other than that, it felt undamaged. He did the same on the right. Searing pain followed. He couldn't remember ever feelin' a hurt that bad. Then he flexed his shoulders. Here was agony equal or greater.

The pain came in waves, crashing through his body from top to bottom. As he forced his muscles to relax, the weight of the earth and the confines of the space began to take its toll. His pulse raced, and he gritted his teeth, terrified at not being able to move.

Anger momentarily blotted out the overwhelming fear. Is this how things worked? He'd finally scraped together a little money, thought this might be the best season of his life, and now it could be his last. And then there was Blind Deer, a woman who piqued his interest, one he wanted to know better, get closer to. In kaleidoscope fashion, one dreadful picture after another rampaged through Kade's mind—plunging him into a full blown panic. What if he made it through only to live forever a stoved-in crippled?

The muffled sound of Tucket's voice and Maggie's barking penetrated the dark tomb, bolstering his spirits and snapping his thoughts back to the present. They would get him out. His breathing slowed, and to ease his soul he grasped at the most comforting notion he could think of—Blind Deer, so beautiful among the meadow of flowers. And what about the kiss they'd shared, innocent yet charged with hope as well as the desire for more.

Usually thoughts of Blind Deer sent his body and mind into a tailspin, encouraging him to do and say things he'd never even considered before. Now the vision quieted his fears, and he smiled, not minding the taste of dirt in his mouth.

The sound of earth and rock tumbling downward gave little warning before more weight crushed in on him—the helpless sensation rushed back full force.

An odd roaring noise filled his head, and a tingling started in his hands and feet, creeping upward along his limbs. He felt weightless as if floating in water. Is this how the beaver felt when they drowned in his traps? A great sorrow welled up in him. He'd never looked at things from their point of view. Never dwelled upon what happened between setting the trap and stretching the hide.

The blackness thickened, covering him with an almost sympathetic embrace. His lungs screamed for air, his body screamed for freedom, his brain simply screamed.

****

Watching as Tucket gingerly approached the dark abyss, Blind Deer inched her horse and the string of animals as close as she dared.

Unafraid when it came to helping his friend, Tucket went right to the edge, risking himself in an attempt to see how bad-off Kade might be. When he stared down into the rift and swore an oath strong enough to uncurl buffalo hair, her worst fears were realized.

Maggie barked and whined and paced along the jagged lip of the hole. Cut off from her master, coyote/dog seemed confused as well as frightened.

The horses and mules, less jumpy now, gave Blind Deer incentive to dismount and tie them securely to a section of nearby trees. Then ignoring Tucket's order to stay put, she edged toward the rift.

Still hovering on the edge, Tucket motioned her back with one hand. "Hold on there, missy. Don't come any closer."

"How bad is it? Does he live?"

"I can't tell. He's too deep to reach from up top. He's under a layer of dirt and rubble. We better get down there fast. You willin' to help?"

"Yes, of course." Again disobeying his words, she crept forward on hands and knees and knelt at his side.

Apparently distracted by his worry over Kade, Tucker did not challenge her defiance in disobeying him. "I knew you'd come through for us, little gal. I might could jump right on down there. But even with the mule a helpin' it be tricky doin's for you to haul Kade or me back up. So, it looks like you're gonna be the one goin' over the side."

As he spoke Tucket eased backward and into an upright position. She scrambled to do the same. Without another word, he set off to get what they might need for the rescue attempt.

Her chest tightened at the thought of going into the dark cleft, but she didn't have time to dwell on the horror as Tucket quickly returned with a few lengths of rope and Hattie, his favorite mule.

"Young Kade will be all right. He's a tough one." Holding her by one arm, he guided Blind Deer to the opposite side of the caved in hole.

"If we go over the edge t'other side by Kade, we could send more of the wall down atop him. We'll go down here offin' this rocky ridge part. It appears more stable and I don't think they dug back this far.

"Who are they?" She waited for an answer as Tucket expertly bound the pieces of rope together.

"They be the lazy bastards who made that hole without properly shoring it up. I think Kade's in a cache, a place to store hides and supplies underground. By the smell of it, somebody tunneled in from the inside of an old painter's den. Unmarked and poorly made, them caches become snares just awaitin' for an unlucky man or animal to happen by."

A cougar den... She glanced around. Did the big cat watch them from afar? Hopefully, it wouldn't approach with coyote/dog around.

"Well, gal, the rope's ready. Are you?" Tucket touched her shoulder as he spoke.

With visions of a hungry panther fresh in her mind she jumped, and then stared into the small black pit. The crater seemed to laugh at her like a greedy mouth waiting to gobble her up. She didn't know if she could do this. Then she decided it couldn't be worse than her time spent in the root cellar at the missionary school. After a while, she'd made friends with the dark, or at least they had called a respectful truce. And what about McCauley? He could be dying as she stood by trying to dredge up enough courage to help him. He was the one trapped, not her—at least not anymore.

Taking one end of the rope from Tucket's hand, she slipped it around her waist allowing him to tie the complex knots he was so good at. He secured the other end of the hemp to the saddle of his mule.

"The rope is strong?" Falling into the hole sounded even worse than being lowered down slowly.

"It's from my seafaring days and has served me well."

"And the knot is tight."

"Tighter than the bark on a tree. It'll hold, Blind Deer. I ain't gonna let anything happen to you."

Believing a white man's word did not come easily. But Sir Reginald hadn't played her false, and for some reason she trusted Tucket too. Gingerly sitting, she dangled her feet over the edge and gripped the rope with white-knuckled hands. Eyes closed, she nodded she was ready.

Tucket eased her forward, the ledge disappeared from beneath Blind Deer, and she dangled alongside the wall.

"I know it's frightful, but you're doin' fine." Although positioned right above her head, Tucket's encouraging words sounded far away. "It would be a might helpful, however, if you were to open your eyes. Then you could see to brace yourself along the wall with your feet. Less chance then of scrapin' up against rocks and tree roots." As he spoke, Tucket maneuvered the mule closer. The rope jerked hard and quick, dropping her about a foot.

Eyes wide, she shifted to avoid a sharp stone. She needed to get this over with. "Hurry, Tucket. He has already been down here much too long." As if waiting for her reassurance he lowered away. Carefully directing her feet, she landed on a small patch of solid ground off to one side. One of Kade's moccasins showed through the dirt, giving her hope he was not buried too deeply.

"Kade, Kade. Can you hear me?" She had never spoken his given name out loud, always just in her heart. She should have, because now only cold silence was the reply.

"Blind Deer." Tucket and the dog peered down at her. Their image didn't test the boundaries of her good vision, but the spot of blue behind them seemed a world away. "Shovel coming down." He dropped the tool. It stuck in the ground handle-up.

She reached for it then hesitated. What if utilizing the sharp-edged tool she accidently added to his injuries. Covered with dirt, it was impossible to know in what position his body lay. Abandoning the idea, she knelt and dug with her bare hands.

As she tore at the earth, millet bugs and worms squirmed between her fingers. When she reached one of Kade's shoulders, renewed hope had her working faster to free his face. His body felt so cold. Was it the chill of the surrounding earth, or were the hands of death already upon him?

Keep going. Dig faster—dig harder.

His body was mostly uncovered. Why didn't he move? Pushing aside the hood of the capote, she felt for a breath of air—nothing. She tugged at his shoulder, partially turning him from his stomach to his side. She pressed her mouth to his, willing her life into him. No response. She pushed at him several times as if to wake him up. She kissed him again, harder, longer, mentally calling him back from the blackness. This time he gasped and a weak current of air escape his mouth.

"Tucket, he lives—but barely."

Smoothing Kade's hair back from his face, she felt a large swelling on the side of his head. That would explain his lack of response—he wandered in the nether-lands. They must get him topside and return to the cabin. She clawed and ripped at the remaining rocks, roots, and dirt, refusing to surrender this man to the last of the earth holding him prisoner.

As she dug deeper, dirt turned to mud. Her hands, covered in cuts and scrapes, soon ached and stung. Did the moisture coating them come from the water or her blood?

When she touched Kade's right leg, he cried out, but the shock of the pain did not drag him back to the conscious world. Perhaps all for the best.

"Kade, my brave warrior, can you hear me? I am sorry to hurt you, but I must secure this rope around you."

But how? She tried lifting just his shoulders and upper torso. His scream rent the air, and a spasm tore through his body.

"I'm sorry, I'm sorry." His injury must be worse than she'd suspected.

She sat back on her heels. He was too heavy for her

to lift, and no amount of weeping or wishing would change that truth. *"You do not need good eyes to see with your brain. Consider all possibilities."* The words of Standing Wolf, her grandfather, called to her. He had taught her strength did not always win the battle. But courage, stealth, and cleverness could overcome great adversity, even her bad vision. Thoughts of his wisdom were cut short as the wall released a torrent of dirt and stones.

Instinctively she leaned over Kade, shielding his head and face, the debris pouring down upon her back. When the small landslide finished, she shook off the dirt and grabbing her braid, Blind Deer used the end to carefully brush the dirt from his closed eyes and mouth.

She must get Kade out of here in all haste. Picking at the knots, she untied the safety rope from around her waist. "Tucket? I need one stout stick, and two of the fattest beaver hides you have. Do you hear me?"

"I hear ya, gal. How long a stick are ya needin'?"

"One almost as long as your leg. And hurry, Tucket, he is very weak and cold."

While she waited, Blind Deer dug a tunnel beneath Kade at waist level. Then she threaded the lifeline of hemp through from side to side. Just as she finished, the hides tumbled down from above.

"Stay put now," Tucket instructed. "The stick be a comin' next, and I don't want to go skewerin' ya or Kade in the process of gettin' it down there."

Close to where she crouched, a straight branch, about the size of her wrist and the proper length, speared the earth like a perfectly thrown war lance.

After checking again to make sure Kade was still breathing, she folded the hides and laid them along his ribs, one on each side of his body. Hopefully they would cushion him when Tucket hauled him up. Grabbing the tail of rope, she pulled through an extra length, and using the knife from her tack belt, she cut off the hemp, dividing the piece into two equal lengths. The remainder of the rope could now be tied off around the hides at his middle.

She straightened the injured limb, relieved when no sound of bone crunching or grating met her ears. Then with the extra rope, she secured the branch along Kade's leg, careful to avoid the cut on his thigh. As she worked, he remained still as death. Had he slipped farther into the realm beyond her reach?

"Tucket?" She tugged on the rope to signal him. "All is ready but pray go gently. He is battered as a sapling after a great storm."

"Stand by." Tucket's image disappeared. "Come on, old girl," he crooned to his mule. "Nice and slow. Step on back now."

The rope went taut, dragging Kade's limp body from the earth. It tore at her heart as he bumped and scraped along. Clambering to her feet, she tried to help guide him up the wall until he was out of reach. After he disappeared over the edge to safety, she breathed a sigh of relief.

No longer moving, her feet went numb inside the stiff wet moccasins, and her hands did not fare much better. She too needed to return to the light. Hurry Tucket, hurry. What was taking so long?

Painful memories escaped the corner of her mind relegated to nightmares, and cold as a winter's wind, they swooped down upon her. Old Lady Dalrymple's face flashed before her, and memories of dread and helplessness swirled around Blind Deer like water—water that felt on the rise. The woman's cruel laugh seemed to echo off the mud walls as the Reverend humiliated and chastised her, promising eternal damnation.

"Do you hear me?"

Did God now summon her from His Kingdom in heaven? In the dark and the damp, lost to her imaginings, it seemed all too real.

"Blind Deer? Ahoy I say, do ya hear me? Grab hold, and I'll hoist ya up."

Coming to her senses, she glanced around, and with hands marked with blood, she freed Kade's rifle from the dirt, and retrieved the rope hanging within arm's reach. Bless Tucket—he'd already looped and knotted it for her. She slipped the ring of hemp over her head and up under her arms. At her signal, he hauled away.

Rising up from the tomb-like realm, she wondered how many times a person could be reborn? At the top, she flopped over like a river otter, gulping in the clean air, basking in the sun.

Tucket dragged her off to one side. The edge of dirt upon which she'd lain collapsed with a rumble, and a large portion of earth and rock spewed into the opening, blotting out the space she had previously occupied. They had both gotten out just in time. She shuddered at what could have happened and crawled over to Kade.

Chapter Eight

It seemed weeks, not days, since they'd cobbled together a travois and hauled Kade back to the cabin.

Blind Deer tried all the medicine she knew to comfort and heal him, and although his fever burned less hot, he wandered back and forth between this world and the next. His recovery would take time—time they did not have to spare. Someone had to get the trade goods to rendezvous.

Last night Tucket and she had discussed the situation. She thought the matter resolved, but as she stood near the corral in the chill morning air, Tucket's expression indicated otherwise.

"We will be fine." Did she sound convincing? Her promise was built more on bravado than conviction. Tucket remained silent.

Since their recent ordeal, the three of them were bound together in such a special way, it seemed unnatural for any one of them to be separated from the other two. But she could not take the furs to trade. Tucket had to go.

"Well, at least there be plenty of firewood." Tucket chuckled and glanced around. "I remember the mornin' young Kade chopped that wood."

"Me too." Blind Deer's neck and cheeks burned hot at the memory of not only the day, but the kisses they had shared.

"I will take good care of him, Tucket."

"On that there ain't no doubt in my mind, Blind Deer. You risked your life for him goin' down into that hole. I expect you'll do right by him again should the need arise."

Still the man hesitated.

"The elk hanging in the meat house will feed us well, and no one will bother us out here. They will all be racing you to rendezvous. Now go before it is too late to start today. And may the God of your choice go with you."

Mounted on Hattie, Tucket sat staring at the cabin. Kade had rallied yesterday, and Tucket had said his goodbyes, although it had been hard to tell if Kade understood the full meaning of things.

The older man reached down and chucked her under the chin. "You be one of the family now, gal. That means I'm leavin' behind the two people in this world most important to me. I'll never forgive myself if anything happens to either one of you."

"And Kade will never forgive either of us if you don't get the best price for those hides. Please go."

She handed Tucket the lead to the string of mules and HBC horses going with him. Before he could see the tears in her eyes, Blind Deer swatted the rump of his mule, sending the animal and Tucket on their way. Having any tears left came as a surprise. Just to look at Kade made her weep.

Tucket turned around once. "Keep your powder dry," he called, giving her a wave goodbye. Then his steadfast form blurred and disappeared.

She stood alone beneath a tall pine, the quiet seeping in all around her until it blanketed everything, but not with warmth. The hair at the back of her neck prickled, and she ran for the cabin.

Stoking the fire, she set a kettle of water to boil to use for tending the wound on Kade's thigh—and for a cup of tea to bolster her strength.

Drinking tea was one of the few white man's customs she enjoyed. And drinking tea in the wilderness especially made her smile. She liked to sip it from a dented tin cup, often-times sitting on the front porch, feet up, her clay pipe in the other hand. What would those prim, white gloved, fancy teacup-toting ladies of St. Louis think of that? The very idea brightened her mood, until she returned to Kade's bedside.

His skin felt too warm again. She washed his face and neck with cool water, and then made a willow bark infusion for him. She worried over him like a mother with a sick child. He was becoming too important in her life. In the end caring for someone brought heartache.

Having been torn away from everyone she'd ever loved, the pain ran deep, almost too deep to rise above. Would Kade also be snatched from her side? Would she lose him too? Could she survive another loss?

One fist raised in the air, she stood in the center of the cabin and defied the fates. "I will not give him up." She all but screamed out the words. When no signs of retribution struck her down, her shoulders relaxed, and cup in hand she returned to Kade's side.

Like a sculpted statue, he lay unmoving. Thank goodness he took what liquid she forced between his lips, but these miniscule feedings could not sustain him for long.

"McCauley, open your eyes and come back to me."

She spoke encouragingly as she set the empty cup aside, and gathered items to see to his injuries, "I am running out of amusing things to talk about. I may have to sing to you—and I have been told my singing is comparable to the sounds of a marauding crow. Not very poetic, but a most enlightening picture."

With supplies she would need arranged nearby, she drew the covers down to his waist and gently massaged the bruised flesh on his shoulder. After she twisted it back into place, the swelling had gone down considerably. She had seen the elders do the same for one of her brothers following his fall from a horse. At least Kade's shoulder should heal properly.

Her hand drifted across his body, her fingers tracing his muscled chest. "I once saw a white man with so much hair he resembled a beast. You could have woven a blanket just from the hair on his back. Never have I seen that among the people of my tribe. This leads me to believe the Salishan have progressed further beyond the animals. But do not worry—you have just the right amount of fur."

Her gaze slid lower. What would it be like to caress him in other places? She might be uncertain as to how her heart felt about Kade, but she knew exactly how her body felt about the man. For those few moments when he'd held her close and kissed her, desire had overruled common sense. This feeling held great power. It was new—it was dangerous.

Keeping him modestly covered, she tended the wound on his right thigh, already showing signs of healing. But the leg remained worrisome. Although not broken, at least not that she could tell, it had been unnaturally twisted. Tucket and she had straightened it before applying a new splint. Now she loosened the straps holding the sticks. There was much bruising, and while his forehead often felt too hot, his leg felt too cold. She rubbed the muscles with a sage and mullein infused oil, massaging deeply, sometimes none too gently, trying to bring a more healthy color to the skin.

"*Ow*. That hurts."

She jumped back, one hand pressed to her chest to calm her fiercely beating heart.

"By the saints they made me pray to, you scared me half to death. How do you feel?"

"My leg hurts, but somehow feels dead, and I can't move it. What in blue blazes happened?"

"Tucket says a cache connected to the den of a mountain cat collapsed, taking you deep into the ground. You hit your head, cut your thigh, dislocated your shoulder, and twisted your leg."

"Is that all? The way I feel I thought maybe I was also dragged behind a mule for a mile or two."

"You were. That is how we got you back to the cabin." She re-tied the splint, leaving his thigh uncovered. "Do not worry. Except for many bruises the rest of you appears very fit."

As the tone and meaning of her words sank in, Kade ran his left hand down beneath the covers. He was stark naked.

"Did you like what you saw?"

"I think it would have been more fun had you been awake."

At her answer, Kade raised a brow as if in surprise, then gave a little smile.

"Where is Tucket?" Apparently Kade didn't remember saying goodbye, and his voice, now filled with worry, sounded weaker.

"He left this morning, taking the hides to the gathering."

"Not alone. He shouldn't go alone."

When he tried to rise, she placed a restraining hand on Kade's chest.

"There was no choice. You are still far from ready to travel."

He fell back onto the bed, pale and exhausted, illustrating her point.

"Three days have passed since your injury. It was a hard decision—a brave decision. Your friend did not wish to leave you."

Shifting her attention back to his thigh, she sprinkled pulverized roots of yellow dock on the laceration, followed by conifer resin. He gave a little yelp, and his leg twitched. The stinging of the medicine should momentarily take his mind off Tucket. And the movement was a good sign. Not all feeling had left the extremity.

When he remained silent, she glanced at his face. He stared back, his eyes overly bright, his cheek flushed. Fever still remained their enemy. She remembered the shaman who would dance come the winter, praying and singing for hours, sometime days, gathering their power then healing the sick. If only one of them were here. She had no such ability and could not even build a suitable sweat lodge to drive the illness from him.

Bandaging the leg injury with a strip of clean cotton, she drew the covers up to his chin. "You need more willow bark. And if you stay awake, you can eat more than tea."

"How is it you're so handy at doctoring people?" He rallied and appeared more alert.

This was a good memory at least. "My grandmother took me into the mountains one summer. I was barely old enough to expertly ride and care for my pony. For three days we ate nothing but what the forest gave us. She taught me of the herbs and plants and how to use them.

"She told me stories about the old days. We grew very close. She prayed for my spirit guide to visit me during our journey, but he did not come. She said not to blame myself. It was not my fault I was only half Indian.

"Then growing up, my mother taught me of the white man's medicine. She told me her God didn't care if I was only half white."

"I remember now you telling me and Tucket about your momma being white." He sighed. "And that's where you got those beautiful green eyes." Almost a whisper, his last words sounded like something he'd pondered before.

"My eyes are a color prized among my people. But they were no gift to me. I cannot see well." There, she'd done it, revealed her greatest weakness.

He didn't appear surprised. "I wondered that day by the river. And the name is a pretty big hint."

She laughed at his teasing. "Maybe I should have stuck with Belinda Dearborn. The name the missionaries gave me."

"No. Promise you won't. That's not who you are. Besides, I like Blind Deer."

His words pleased her greatly. She tried not to let it show. "Tucket is an unusual name. Is it not?"

"Indeed it is. Kind of short for the fact he spent a lot of time in Nantucket. Truth be told, he's from Louisiana. But he keeps that a secret, fearing folks might shorten that too, and call him Louise."

She couldn't decide whether that could be true, or if Kade was just trying to make her laugh. He seemed to enjoy doing so. A good quality in a man.

"How did your mother come to live with your tribe?"

He was also very inquisitive—maybe not such a good quality. But Kade's honesty about how he'd lost his family and met Tucket, gave her the confidence to open up, at least a little. The idea of telling the tale to Kade in comparison to telling Lord Seton felt completely different—back then an act of desperation, now a gift of sharing.

****

"Well I'm not surprised the Blackfoot were involved." Kade shook his head then added, "She sounds like one courageous lady. Did the thought of leaving never enter her mind?"

Why did everyone always ask that?

"Never. She was happy, with a brave husband and three strong sons. Then they had me. The willful child. I did not wish to come out head first."

"I guess you were wayward and independent from the very beginning." Some of his words were slurred, and he closed his eyes.

"Yes. Now you must finish the tea and rest."

With encouragement, he finished a second cup of willow bark tea, and when she added another blanket to comfort him, he dozed off almost immediately. She fetched the last of the hot water and made herself a cup of tea. Sitting in a chair beside him, she sipped and pondered. Never before had she trusted anyone enough to reveal so much of her life.

After a while, Kade became restless, and knowing her voice calmed him, she rambled on about whatever came to mind.

"My brothers all favored father—no one would mistake them for anything but Indian. But I favored mother. My hair is not true black, and it curls when it rains." She rose and collected Kade's buckskins and her sewing bundle. "My thoughts were often troubled as I tried to live in both worlds—two languages, two religions, two ways of thinking and being. I wished there had been two of me like my twin brothers. Each of my parents loved me, and I wished to please them both."

Returning to the chair, she put awl and sinew to use, salvaging Kade's linen shirt and repairing the seams in his leather pants. The ones they cut apart when they removed his clothing. But he needed new moccasins. His old ones were worn thin—and they smelled of rot and death from the panther den. She would start on those tomorrow.

As she worked, she glanced around the little cabin. "And now I am here." Her words came out in a gentle sigh. "Unable to find my people—and unwilling to return to the East. Once again, I am lost between two worlds."

"Not lost, Blind Deer," Kade mumbled. "I found you."

****

Tucket glanced back one last time at the towering white peaks reaching for the sky and the lodgepole pines standing sentry on the trace. He sure felt bad leavin' Kade and Blind Deer behind.

Hopefully the side of elk would hold them over until Kade was up and about. It hadn't been a very big animal. Had it been wrong turning a portion of it into jerky for the trail? He'd be to rendezvous in four or five days. There was bound to be game along the way. But with the possibility of unfriendlies around, it was best not to be drawing attention to one's self by clamoring about and throwin' fire without good cause.

Too late now anyway.

He faced forward and hunched down into the saddle. The hooves of his mule made soft rhythmic thuds on the trail, and the horses and pack animals added their various jingles and jangles to the song of their passing.

Beyond the muted sounds of animals and forest, a silence settled over everything like a layer of morning fog. Solitude—the one thing he'd missed during his years of whaling. Even though the view from the rail could be the loneliest thing a man could imagine, on a ship full of sailors, a man could never be alone. He was glad to be on dry land.

The taking of those behemoths was nasty business, and hard on the soul. He was starting to feel the same way about beavering. Killing an animal for food was one thing but killing to keep some rich bastard's head warm back East was another.

Things was getting crowded too. Used to be a man could wander about out here and rarely cross paths with another human being. And the year was measured by the comings and goings of the moon and the changing of the seasons. Now it was near impossible to find a hole Man hadn't ruined with his greasy handprint. And the beaver weren't the only thing disappearing. The Indian tribes were growing smaller from warring with the white man, and accordingly less friendly.

He never thought he'd see the day when westerin' sounded more and more like a good idea. He'd heard tell the Oregon territory was something to behold—maybe it was time.

As the animals settled into an easy walk, his mind drifted. It had been a long while since this child had traveled on his lonesome. Him and Kade had shared the trail for many a year, and good ones at that—shinin' times. He smiled, recalling the scrawny boy delivered into his hands by fate. Once Kade came to grips with the loss of his family, he'd worked hard at becoming a man. Always asking questions, always wanting to learn something new, most always wanting to do things his own way.

He couldn't imagine not being with Kade, although now there was Blind Deer to consider. They made a good match, if they could but see the obvious. Would they cotton to the idea of maybe heading west too?

Tucker revisited old adventures in his mind and thought about what the future might hold, and the morning slipped into afternoon. Then he came to attention as the path up ahead narrowed and dipped downward—a good place for an ambush. Hattie snorted and swung her head to the right, and the string of animals behind him started mincing steps and tossing heads. Something was coming through those trees. Bear, painter, wolf?

Indians.

He kept a steady pace—one hand on the loaded

pistol shoved in his belt. With any luck they were Shoshone. He knew quite a few words and signs to palaver with several tribes, and the Shoshone had treated him fair in the past. Of course, alone and laden with beaver plews, he was an easy mark. If they were Siksika he was a goner—the Blackfoot weren't much on tradin' or makin' small talk.

A party of four men filed out of the timber. Crow—big strapping lads, outfitted with bows and arrows, two of them also carrying spears. They appeared amiable—so far.

Tucket offered words of peace, mentioning a Crow chief's name he'd traded with before. Just like in the city, sometimes it was who you knew that counted, more than what you knew.

They all eyed one another. Three of the braves assessed his packs and accoutrements. The apparent leader urged his horse forward blocking the trail. It wasn't hot, but Tucket began to sweat while a wonderin' what they were thinking.

The Crow loved horses—theirs and everybody else's. Their penchant for them was known far and wide. They seemed to look upon accumulating animals as a challenge, or kinda the way they made their living. He cut loose the HBC mounts captured the day they found Blind Deer and made a sign he was gifting them to the men. Then he held up the bag of jerky and tossed the food to the closest brave.

The four Indians exchanged glances, and words he couldn't quite catch. As nervous as if he waited for a hang fire, Tucket tried to remain calm. Finally, the Crow blocking the path backed up his mount, indicating for him to proceed.

Touching his heels to Hattie, Tucket gave a friendly nod, and ambled off with the pack animals. Would the horses and food be enough? He hoped by not showing fear he would win their mercy—and not an arrow in his back.

His mountain man luck held. They allowed him to pass unmolested. Indians was hard to figure. On another day he might have gone under, or at least be robbed blind. Not wasting time or daylight, when they were out of sight, he picked up the pace, putting as many miles between him and the Crow braves as possible.

It was strange doin's in the wilderness, where keepin' alive could depend just as much on one moment of providence as on a lifetime of learnin'.

Chapter Nine

Kade opened his eyes to morning light—which morning he had no idea. Had it been last night or last week when he'd laid half-conscious listening to Blind Deer's life story—or at least the parts she was willing to reveal to him.

Turning his head, he searched the cabin for a glimpse of her. His effort was rewarded with a lightning bolt of pain shooting through his skull. An involuntary moan escaped him, and his stomach lurched. Sleeping had done him no good—he felt worse not better. The dizziness increased, and he closed his eyes. Except for the day Tucket saved his life, he couldn't remember ever feeling so sick and weak.

The bed jiggled. Then a cold wet nose pressed against his bare shoulder. Cautiously, he smiled, but he didn't open his eyes or move to pet the dog, both efforts sounding too costly.

"Maggie," he croaked through parched lips. "Hello girl. Go find Blind Deer."

"I am here, McCauley." Blind Deer crossed the room, the jingling of beads and shells growing more distinct. She touched his brow.

"Your fever is down." She sounded much relieved by this fact.

"I hope you are planning to stay with us for a while this time? You have been very poor company, coming and going with no advanced notice. I have had to keep up both sides of the conversation. Not an easy task."

"How long have I been out this time?"

"Another two days."

"Holy heck, I'd better get up." He made to rise, struck down once more when the room tilted and spun at a crazy angle.

"You are feeling dizzy?"

"Like a 'possum in a barrel rolling downhill."

"You need food." He fell back upon the pillows. "Tucket shot a young elk before he left. He took some, and the rest is in the meat house. I will bring in the best pieces and prepare something more than soup to strengthen your blood."

Kade heard Blind Deer's movements grow faint and disappear. When he was sure she was gone, he tried once more to get up. Slumped over and blurry-eyed, he sucked in a deep breath and made it to the edge of the bed. His shoulder and rib cage painfully rebelled, and he exhaled slowly and with trepidation. Wasn't there any part of his body still working like it was supposed to?

So far, each little movement was a misery and his head was beginning to throb worse than ever. He sure was a pitiful excuse for a man today, and he wasn't good at being helpless. In fact, he was downright prideful when it came to admitting frailty of any kind. He gave himself no quarter, and to have his own body beyond his control seemed the ultimate betrayal.

He had to get up and get himself and Blind Deer to rendezvous.

Standing, he felt quite pleased with himself. Walking was another matter altogether. The unwieldy splint and the weakness in his one leg were a lethal combination. He spun around and barely made it back before falling face down on the bed.

****

Kade's return to consciousness was encouraging. Although still dizzy, he sounded much stronger. Now what he needed was encouragement and good food.

Her happiness faded when she noticed the door to the meat house stood ajar, the wood at the bottom gnawed and broken, the earth in front dug up and scattered. Running the last few steps, she peered inside. As her eyes adjusted to the dark interior, her gaze took in the elk on the floor, torn to bits and scattered about in the dirt. A distinctly rancid smell told Blind Deer the reason for the destruction.

The wolverine snarled and turned to face her full on. His mouth a collection of long white teeth, shining bright even in the dim light. She threw the cook pot she carried at him and drew her knife. The metal container bounced harmlessly off the creature's back, but the noise seemed to startle him for the moment. Blind Deer backed away. If she could make it back to the cabin, she'd be okay. Then her left foot came down on a twig, and the loud snap triggered the beast into action.

With a hideous snarl, he lunged forward. She slammed the door shut, feeling his weight smash up against the other side. Claws ripping and tearing, he extended one big paw through the hole he'd dug in the dirt at the bottom of the wooden panel. Still leaning against the door, she bent over and stabbed at his foot with her knife. He yelped and pulled back—she turned and ran.

Reaching the cabin, she stopped and looked back.

She was safe. The wolverine hadn't followed. He seemed content with the ruined elk so readily available. Dog barked inside. Should she turn her loose? Tangling with a wolverine, the outcome would be anybody's guess, and it would serve no purpose. The food was ruined.

What was she going to do now? She couldn't tell Kade. Knowing they were without food would concern him all the more. But he needed meat, and he needed it now.

There was only one answer. She would go hunting. Something she had never done before. When she was on her own, camas roots, vegetables, and berries kept her going, along with buying or trading for more substantial fare. Could she do this?

Slipping inside, she searched for an excuse to explain her delay in making Kade the promised meal. She needn't have worried. He lay sprawled across the bed, unconscious again and full of fever. Obviously, he'd tried to get up and it had cost him dearly. She struggled to rearrange him in a normal sleeping position. Male pride was not good medicine.

Before he had taken his leave, Tucket had shown her how to load Kade's longrifle. Powder, patch, ball—powder, patch, ball. As she located both powder horns and shooting pouch, she chanted the three words over and over as if they formed a sacred litany. If she got the order incorrect the rifle would not fire, or worse yet a ball could be stuck, rendering the rifle either useless or ready to explode when the trigger was pulled.

Ugh. The Kentucky rifle weighed more than she remembered. Stock down, muzzle up she balanced the weapon against her body, and hands shaking, she measured out the black pepper-like granules. Down the barrel it went, then tapping the side, she settled the powder.

With the patch knife, she cut off a small square of cotton shirting and sucked on the fabric to moisten the material. Her mouth was so dry she barely had enough spit to wet the tiny piece of linen. As saturated as it was likely to get, she laid the square flat across the muzzle. Carefully balancing a lead ball on top, sprue facing upward, she used the short starter to seat the ball.

After realigning the wooden implement, she pounded on it with the flat of her palm, painfully catching the webbing between her thumb and forefinger as the wood connected with the lip of the muzzle. Blood ran down her hand. How in the name of all her ancestors was she going to shoot anything when she couldn't even load the gun without getting hurt?

She wiped her hand on her leather dress—the blood of a warrior, what a joke. Using the ramrod, she drove the ball down the barrel until it settled firmly. Weighed down with the powder horns, shooting pouch, a rope, and the rifle, she forced herself upright and shuffled over to Kade. Giving him one last look, she left the cabin.

She wanted to shoot the wolverine, if for nothing else than for revenge, or to release her fear and anger. But he was only trying to stay alive, and his flesh would be stringy and tainted by musk and the odor of the carrion he generally ate. When the food was gone, he would wander off.

****

Trekking through the woods for hours revealed only one game trail, but no large animals, or even a rabbit. Nothing moved in the area around Blind Deer. She usually saw all manner of creatures—some even came to her willingly. But then her intent had been friendly, now she sought to kill them. Somehow, they knew.

As she trudged along, the longrifle seemed to grow in weight and length, getting caught on brambles and branches, slowing her progress and making noise. Each step became a conscious effort—soon even the tiniest of stones tripped her up, and crossing a fallen log became almost insurmountable. In her tribe, hunting was not a woman's right. Were the Spirits angry at her for trying? When the daylight waned, adding to her poor vision, she returned to the cabin empty handed.

****

For two more days, she repeated the grueling ritual, from sun up to sun down. Meanwhile, Kade grew weaker. He was dying. Tea, water, and flapjack crumbs couldn't keep a healthy man alive, let alone heal a body as badly hurt as his had been. Tired and near starving herself, wild unchecked thoughts ran through her mind, and finding food became her dark obsession. What she wouldn't give for a buffalo hump roast with prairie butter. Or even the spring shoots of balsamroot, the famine-food which had once saved her tribe following a brutal winter.

On the third morning, weak and dizzy, she sat down on a log, the loaded rifle across her lap. Maggie sat several yards away staring at her. The dog would willingly die for Kade. With this realization, a horrifying idea took form. A failure at hunting the white man's way, maybe she should use Indian logic.

Blind Deer put powder in the flash pan, closed the

frizzen, and cocked the hammer back. Bringing the rifle up to her shoulder, she fought to keep the heavy barrel from wavering as she brought the sights in line with dog's head. The dog stared at her with trusting blue eyes, canting its head to one side as if questioning her actions. Blind Deer took a deep breath, held it, and pulled the trigger.

Smoke filled the air, and the recoil nearly knocked her over backward. The ball smacked into a pine tree off to the left of Maggie. The dog yelped and ran through the woods—not once looking back.

The rifle slid from her grip to the ground. She covered her face with her hands and sobbed, tears flowing unchecked. Sick at heart, she rocked back and forth. At the last moment, she had pulled to the side. What was she thinking? She couldn't shoot dog. She looked too much like Coyote—the gods would never forgive her. And besides, her mother had been called Maggie, at least by her father.

Weak with the need for food, her mind wandered, and sitting up straight, her hands in her lap, a sad smile reached her lips. Mother had been so full of life, singing little songs under her breath, chattering on about the books she'd read and things she'd seen. Father had dubbed her his Magpie, which eventually became Maggie. A nice memory, perhaps even a good excuse for not shooting dog, but it didn't put meat in the pot.

After resting a bit, Blind Deer rallied, and using her last bit of strength and gumption, she headed back to Kade. Along the way, she checked the bird nest she'd noticed earlier and gathered the broken bits of shell. Even these would hold nourishment.

Several yards from her destination, she stopped

dead in her tracks.

Someone had been at the cabin.

Chapter Ten

Three wild ducks, dead, cleaned, and nestled in a bed of grass lay in front of the cabin door. Fear crushed her relief at seeing the food. Was it done out of kindness—or bait?

She tightened her grip on the empty rifle and glanced around in all directions. She should have reloaded while out in the woods. Another lesson learned.

Scooping up the ducks, she scrambled inside, slammed the door shut, and stood facing the slab of wood. Her respirations slowed from panting back to normal when it occurred to her someone could be lurking inside. She spun around, her gaze sweeping every nook and corner. Nobody was there except Kade, pale of skin, and labored of breath.

After barring the door, she started a fire in the hearth and cooked the fowl, some roasted, some fried. Regardless of which method, every scrap must be used, including the bones and tendons to be boiled for a hearty broth.

****

It had only been a day and a half, but the hours blurred one into the next, seeming to go on forever as she drifted in the land of purgatory, the haunted realm the Reverend spoke of. She existed between the hellish fear of losing Kade and the heavenly hope of having him return to normal.

Kade grew stronger, eating everything she gave him, but he did not return completely, and it was lonely without dog. Blind Deer wondered if Maggie would ever come home. She called to her several times and set out clean water in the old dented bucket. She even set out a precious scrap of duck for her to eat.

When not fretting over the dog, Blind Deer divided her time between ministering to Kade and wondering— no worrying—about who had left the food for them. Food nearly gone. Should she leave the cabin unattended to try hunting again?

Kade opened his eyes, smiled, then closed them again. Like a flash of lightning, he'd come and gone, and so did her expectations. She repositioned him on his side, the sheep skins piled behind him. Moving him about was good for his lungs and his skin, and so far both remained healthy. She hoped such small gestures were of comfort to him.

As if in answer he mumbled and reached out, and although his eyes remained closed, he instinctively found her wrist as she stood beside the bed. Drawing her hand to his chest, a peacefulness returned to his face. His breathing slowed and he rested easier.

Kade's beard and mustache were of some consequence, the new growth making him appear older. She touched his cheek, just above the hairline, the skin smooth almost tender. Although a rugged man, he had a softer side too, like the kindness he'd shown her.

Not wanting to just stand and stare at him, she broke his grasp and backed away from the bed to begin the daily chores of housekeeping. If she did not stick to a schedule and perform these common rituals, she feared she might lose her mind.

She glanced at the empty bucket by the door. She should at least leave the cabin for water. Never before had the desolation of the prairie or the closed-in darkness of the woods ever intimidated her. The towering mountains and rolling hills and valleys were her home, her refuge. Yet recently, it felt as if eyes watched from afar, and nothing was safe or sacred.

Screwing up her courage, and knowing there was no other choice, Blind Deer set out, bucket in one hand, loaded rifle in the other.

****

Awareness washed over Kade. Eyes closed, he knew he was in his cabin, and he knew the warmth he felt was from the morning sun, not the cold silent hearth.

Cautiously, he felt around on the bed, half expecting Blind Deer to be there, warm and safe. Although he hadn't been able to respond, he knew she lay beside him last night, at least for a little while. But the blankets were cold, the bed empty. Maybe her nearness had been but a dream.

Eyes open, he winced at the daylight but suffered little other pain. In wonderment, he passed his hand across his eyes and through his tangled hair. Images from what he assumed were the past day or two came to mind, but like shards of glass nothing fit together. At least he had improved a great deal since the last time he had returned to full consciousness.

After a deep breath or two, he inched his way closer to the side of the bed. Then slowly, ever so slowly, he slid his legs over the edge until his feet touched the floor. Pushing upright with his arms, he sat motionless except for his gaze. Where was everybody? Both Maggie and Blind Deer were conspicuous in their absence.

The splint was gone, and gaining his feet, he got his bearings and grabbed a blanket off the bed, wrapping the wool around his shoulders and naked body. The short shuffling excursion to the cabin door wore him out a bit, and he leaned against the wall before attempting to go outside.

Where was Blind Deer? The water bucket and rifle were missing. Probably gone down to the stream. She had been at his side since the accident. He remembered hearing her voice and the stories she had told. He remembered fighting to come back to her. She had been his warmth and light. Her spirit his only sanctuary in the fearful world he'd roamed alone.

Opening the cabin door, he stood in the sun, soaking up the healing rays as he awaited her return, a vision to fill his eyes and heart. Instead, an Indian brave materialized before him.

The solitary man stood several yards away, clothed only in leggings, a loin cloth, and moccasins. The man stared back, formidable and unafraid. The white talons of his bear claw necklace glinted in the sun, reminding Kade of another brave and the eagle claw that had ripped his leg open those many years ago. The man's face was slashed with red and black paint, adding a terrifying bit of decoration to the already threatening spectacle.

Armed with a Missouri war axe, bow, and knife, the solitary figure stood stock still, a painted bag at his feet. The feeling he thought himself invincible radiated from his stance and demeanor, although he made no move to attack.

Holy mother of God, what a way to start his first day out of bed. Kade didn't feel fit to take on a lame rabbit let alone an unexpected Indian. As nonchalantly as possible, he glanced around for Blind Deer. Had this man already found her? Did she lie injured or dead nearby? If she were unharmed, he hoped she had the sense to stay hidden.

"Easy, friend." Kade straightened to his full height and tried not to weave about. "We weren't expecting company." He fought to keep the man in focus. "But you're welcome. We've always lived in peace, wishing no harm to anyone, and expecting none to ourselves."

The stranger's reply came first in Indian, and then in French. Unfamiliar with either language, Kade didn't understand the man's intent.

The silence hanging in the air became increasingly uncomfortable, and Kade's strength began to dwindle. Just as passing out seemed a possibility, he sighted Blind Deer approaching from behind their uninvited guest.

Rifle at her shoulder, she moved silently through the grass. When she was a few paces behind the man, she cocked the gun, and call out. The intruder appeared to recognize the language she spoke. From his topknot to his beaded moccasins, the warrior tensed for action and slowly turned around.

Sweat broke out on Kade's forehead. Blind Deer only had one shot, and he had none. If she missed, they would both be dead before either could make a second move. Kade grabbed the door-jam, listening to the conversation flowing between Blind Deer and the stranger—their words did not seem angry. Then to his disbelief, Blind Deer lowered the rifle from her shoulder and put the hammer at half-cock. The expression on her face registered neither fear nor surrender. She stood proud and tall, not twitching a muscle as the Indian stepped closer.

Kade was about to make what he figured would be a fatal attempt at Blind Deer's deliverance when he heard laughter.

The intruder stood at ease, his weapons turned aside. Their words were exchanged with increasing animation, and the Indian reached out and playfully tugged at Blind Deer's hair. Then they spoke quietly for several moments, and the mood surrounding them changed. The man placed one hand on Blind Deer's shoulder as if to console her. She hung her head then swiped at her face with the back of her hand.

Kade stiffened to attention as the man recovered the nearby painted bag and reached inside. A field-dressed wild goose was revealed and offered to Blind Deer. An expression of relief eased across her face. Kade's shoulders relaxed.

The two spoke quietly a few more moments. Then the brave turned to squarely face Kade, his gaze intense. He shook his bow in the air as if in warning, and after a short speech in his own language and a couple of impressive war hollers, exemplifying his prowess, he departed. Not a trembling branch or whisper of sound marked the warrior's return to the forest.

Blind Deer ran toward the cabin. She propped the rifle against the outside wall, and still holding the large bird by its legs, she threw her arms around his neck. The goose thumped across his back sending stray feathers floating through the air. Soft and yielding, her body pressed tight against his. Cocooned in his blanket, he couldn't properly return her hug, but she was safe and that's what mattered. His spirit sighed with relief, and at her closeness, his body ached with need.

Then the moment was over.

Standing on tip-toes, she sweetly kissed his cheek. "Thank the heavens you are back, Kade. At the sight of you upright and looking so well, my heart rejoices." She glanced back over her shoulder. "On the same day in which it has also been badly broken."

Kade grabbed up the rifle and allowed her to help him back inside.

"What do you mean? Who was that man?" He sat on the edge of the bed anxious to understand what was going on.

"He is my brother."

"You mean like part of your tribe?"

"No. I mean my older brother, Nikota. One who playfully tormented, yet always protected me—until I went away."

Stunned, he remained silent, trying to grasp the full meaning of her words. "You should have invited him in."

"I did. He has made camp nearby. He does not trust easily, especially white people. We will talk again soon."

"He had news then of your family, your people?"

"Yes, but the word was not good. Except for a very few, they are all gone."

"Your mother and father?"

She nodded. Her chin quivered, and she turned away, fussing with the goose she had placed upon the cutting board.

He knew what it felt like to lose one's parents. About to say so, a shiver of suspicion took hold of him instead. "How did he know where to find you?" Coincidence was always a possibility, but out here, it was hard enough finding folks on purpose let alone by chance.

"He crossed paths with a small Hudson's Bay Party and their Blackfoot guides. Listening from afar, he heard them talking around the campfire. They groused about having to search for two free trappers and a Flathead Indian woman with green eyes and a bounty on her head.

"The description of the woman caught his attention. The next day, the brigade split up in order to more quickly cover the terrain. My brother approached a lone man in peace but was met with war. He won of course."

There was pride in her voice, but not much else registered with him but one thing. "There's a bounty on your head?"

"Yes. The Reverend has accused me of not only running away, but of stealing from the mission school. The local law is cracking down on *thieving redskins*, so they made a poster of me and offered a reward. They even alerted the Army."

Words he couldn't utter in her presence flooded his mind.

"This is bad doin's. They'll be looking for you at rendezvous. Tarnation, they'll be looking for you everywhere, from here back to the Mississippi."

At his words, the color faded from her cheeks. He hadn't meant to scare her. Better change the subject.

"What was your brother doing out there in the first place?"

"He too is heading for rendezvous, to trade for supplies. He crossed the HBC path by accident. They made so much noise, they were hard to miss. Since peace was not possible, he used cunning and bravery and took them out, one by one. The Blackfoot have always been our enemy, and now the HBC is too. Before the last one died, my brother asked him many questions. Searching for us, they had returned to the very site of the prior battle—where you shot me."

Now it was his turn to feel the lifeblood drain from his face. "You didn't tell him about that did you?"

"Maybe someday, but no, he would probably wish to kill you."

He didn't doubt her words for a moment. "How did he know to look for you?"

"Nikota saw the poster they carried. The drawing of me was true to life and stated a young green-eyed Indian woman with hair that curled was on the run from a missionary school in St. Louis. He felt in his heart it had to be me. Then although the trail was old and the English were too stupid to do so, and the Blackfoot too lazy, he tracked us from the battle site to your cabin."

"But what happened to your tribe?"

Pain and sorrow erased away every bit of happiness at finding her brother.

"They are nearly all gone, wiped out. Nikota seemed reluctant to tell me the whole story. But he hinted the HBC was involved in that too."

Kade stood and reached out with one arm and drew her near. "I'm so sorry, Blind Deer. You were so close to joining them, so close to fulfilling your dream of returning home."

She clung to him, sobbing. Before now, she had never shown any signs of weakness. At least not in front of him or Tucket. Maybe she felt safer knowing her brother was nearby, or maybe she had begun to trust him just a little bit.

"They never got my letters. They never knew how I suffered, or how much I missed them. And I never got theirs."

She pulled away and sniffed. An expression of grim determination replaced her sorrow.

"The English also talked of their Captain. His name is Sulgrave."

Kade had heard the name before. A leader for the Company out of Fort Elise, this booshway had a ruthless reputation for mistreating the British trappers as well as his own men. Men like the soldiers who had originally captured Blind Deer—the ones he and Tucket had killed. Now her brother had killed more of Sulgrave's men, and the Captain would be out for revenge on all of them.

"I must leave for this rendezvous, and then go back to help what few of my people are left. Your condition is much improved. You can stay here on your own. My brother and I will leave in the morning."

"You're not going anywhere without me."

Brother or no brother, alarm shot through him at the thought of her taking off without him. He had to say something to convince her to stay, yet he really had no right to ask her to wait for him. No right to these grand new feelings and the overwhelming need to protect and care for her.

"Besides, you're wrong. If you leave me behind it

would be very bad for my recovery." A lame excuse, and unkind of him to play upon her sympathy—but anything to buy him some time. He couldn't imagine waking up to find Blind Deer gone for good. Couldn't imagine living in a world without her.

"We're partners now. And partners don't turn their backs on one another." The words came out sounding all riled up as the fear of losing her turned to anger. "You didn't abandon me when I got hurt. Don't deny me the right of seeing you safely to the Green."

Her expression sobered even more, and she gazed into his eyes as if divining the true intent behind his words. "We will go together then, McCauley. But not tomorrow. In a few days. If we leave in haste and you sicken on the trail, you are too big for me to carry in a cradleboard." She gave a little chuckle at her own humor.

Blind Deer wasn't inclined to making jokes. Despite her sadness, seeing her brother had brought a new aspect to her personality. Maybe from remembering how life used to be.

"All right then." He nodded in agreement, and the reprieve left him lightheaded. "We'll go in two days."

Standing beside the bed, she put a hand on his shoulder, encouraging him to sit on the edge.

"You must rest now. I will start a fire, and soon we will have roast goose."

Still facing her, Kade let the blanket fall from around his shoulders to his lap. Before she could turn away, he reached out, placing his hands around her waist. She offered him no resistance as he drew her closer, immobilizing her between his still covered thighs. Leaning forward he lay his cheek against the front of her soft buckskin dress—and against her soft tempting woman's body.

When she ran her fingers through his hair, cradling him closer, a powerful yearning took control of him—he couldn't think, only feel, and he reveled in the gentle rise and fall of her chest and the quickening beat of her heart.

"You have recovered more than you let on, McCauley." A breathless quality wrapped around her words. "Perhaps a ploy to draw me unsuspecting to your bed."

"No." He drew back and eased his hold on her. "I'll not trick you into sharing my blankets." Besides, he wanted their first time together to be his best effort, proving the magnitude of his love—and his prowess. Just imagining their bodies united in love set off a collection of body aches overshadowing the need in other parts of his body. Nothing was gonna happen tonight.

"Go cook." The words came out gruffly, and remaining seated, he gently pushed her away. "Go, before I change my mind and really give myself a relapse." He tried to be content watching Blind Deer prepare their meal, but he hungered for her, not for food.

"Where's Maggie?" Suddenly, he remembered he hadn't seen her in what seemed like days.

As Blind Deer bent to add more wood to the fire, she froze mid-motion. Recovering, she finished the task in silence. Standing tall, and dusting the bits of wood from her hands, she turned to face him. Her serious demeanor, and the hurt look in her eyes, had him grabbing the edge of the bed with both hands.

"Is Maggie hurt? What happened?"

"You were dying Kade. We were both starving. All the elk Tucket left was ruined by a greedy wolverine, and except for catching one small fish, my eyes failed me, and I failed you. Try as I did, I couldn't find us any food. There was nothing left to eat—nothing. Do you understand? You were fading. And I despaired. Not thinking straight, I thought Maggie our only hope."

By the grace of the Almighty, had she killed Maggie? Kade lurched upright, one hand instinctively clutching the blanket in place. Had she fed him his own dog? His stomach revolted as the vision took hold. He knew of tribes who ate dog, but he would have rather died than eat Maggie.

"You mean she's dead?" He braced for the answer.

"Oh no, Kade. I could not kill her. At the last minute I fired to one side, hitting a tree, but the noise and betrayal scared her away. I think she is nearby. I left her a scrap of food after we had the ducks which Nikota left for us. I am sorry, Kade. I miss dog too."

"She'll come back." Relief flooded his senses, and he slumped back onto the edge of the bed. "She's been known to go roaming on occasion."

To have considered using Maggie for food, Blind Deer must have been half out of her mind, just like he'd been most of the time. He knew she'd grown fond of the big dog. He tried to imagine her torment deciding between killing the dog and watching him grow weaker, maybe dying.

"You shouldn't have been left here alone to fend for yourself. It's my fault you had to go through this."

"Do not blame yourself. If anyone is a failure it is I. Living with the white man has made me soft. I thought I could survive in the old ways, but I cannot. With each passing day, I realize more and more how much I have changed. I tried hard to remember the teachings from my childhood, but I have forgotten the little things. And lots of little things make a big thing. I must go back and try to help my tribe, but I do not feel like one of them, and I cannot go back East either. I belong nowhere, with no future. I have failed."

There was anger in her voice.

Kade tugged lightly on one arm until she glanced at him. "I remember quite a bit of what you told me as you sat by my bedside. You gave me a glimpse of your soul, and what I saw there was beautiful—despite all the ugliness you've seen. You're not a failure. If anything, you're a testimony to what good you found in either group."

Why couldn't she see her worth, and a future together with him? If it meant following her rather than his own trail, he was willing to give it a try. He was willing to do anything—anything but give Blind Deer up. Somehow, he would make it his mission for the two of them to stay together.

Chapter Eleven

That night, Blind Deer stood barefoot and silent in the dark cabin, sleep eluding her. Kade's slow, even breathing indicated he slumbered undisturbed.

He had made great strides today, and like he promised they would leave soon. They must, and her brother would travel with them. What would Nikota do after rendezvous? The HBC was enemy to her brother now too. They would all be on dangerous ground when they arrived there.

Gazing through the partially shuttered window, she stood transfixed by the netherworld delivered silently during the borrowed time found only in the deep of night. Everything within her view was peaceful and still, unlike the thoughts tearing through her mind.

Nikota's tracking skills and good fortune had reunited them. She also believed it to be an answer to her many prayers to her ancestors. What a joy to see him again. He had been the best possible messenger but bearing the worst possible news.

A cloud passed over the moon, plunging the landscape into darkness, just as the shadow of concern dulled her bright feeling for Kade.

He was becoming too close to her.

During these last few days, they had shared many a tender touch and a few stolen kisses, the true emotion behind these innocent actions mounting to a fevered pitch. The rapture building between them was ripe, ready to flower into a passionate display she may not be able to resist.

Kade would soon be healed enough to approach her with a man's yearning to match her own feminine desire. But surrendering to him physically would be a mistake. Giving him her heart would be an even bigger disaster. So many people she cherished had died, leaving her stricken by their loss. Besides, he was a man who cherished his freedom, and she must return with her brother to her people. Although the survivors were few, they were in great need of help—she would not turn her back on them. This meant she must be content with only Kade's friendship, and not take or give anything greater.

To share one's love the first time was a gift, to be given only once, never to be reclaimed. A precious gift to be treasured and remembered together for all the years to come. But after rendezvous, she must leave Kade. There would be no years to come. Yet what little they could share, if only for a short while, would become a good memory to help defeat the bad ones.

The sky cleared and moonlight streamed in through the window and tiny spaces in the wall where the chinking was missing.

"It's a glorious night."

She gasped in surprise at the sound of Kade's voice. He drew near, his arms encircling her from behind. Held a willing captive, her heartbeat quickened. She pictured his broad chest and strong shoulders, and unable to resist, she leaned back, surrendering to his embrace.

He pressed gentle kisses to her arched neck, his

hands gliding upward from her waist to her breasts—
the thin nightshirt given to her at the Fort created only
an imperceptible barrier. Desire fought reason and
almost won. But he wasn't hers to keep, and being with
him would be dangerous as well as wonderful. What if
she got with child? She could barely take care of
herself.

His right hand trailed lower to the space between
her legs, and thoughts of logic dissolved away when he
groaned out her name and pressed closer from behind—
his need and desire as obvious as her own. She knew
this was wrong. It would make their parting of ways
even more difficult.

"I cannot do what you silently ask of me. I've
never been with a man. This is not my time."

If only she had still been living with her tribe,
wearing a virgin's cape, announcing to all men her
status—making such words unnecessary.

Kade stilled his movements, issuing a sound
between a growl and a groan. She trembled, but not
with anticipation. Mistrust reared its head, and for a
moment she feared his reaction. Did her declaration
anger him? Would he try to have her anyway?

He stood a little straighter, and the cool night air
slipped between them. "Well we're even on that score.
I've never been with a man either."

His attempt at humor quelled her fright. She felt
guilty for thinking he would be so cruel as to force
himself upon her. This time she expected the worst and
found the best.

Remaining at her back and seeming to understand,
he rested his hands upon her shoulders.

"I'm not giving up on us, Blind Deer. I can wait."

When she turned her head to glance back at him, he kissed her cheek, and then reaching for one of her hands, he drew her closer to the window. "The moon is so big tonight it reminds me of a Trapper's Moon."

Blind Deer squinted up at the sky, and although she would never know the patterns formed by the twinkling bits of light, her shortcoming did not stifle her curiosity for the world around her.

"What exactly is a Trapper's Moon?" She was glad they pursued a subject other than the history of her love life, or lack thereof. And she enjoyed hearing about anything to do with Saka'am, the moon.

"It comes in February, and it's a formidable sight—big and bright, like a golden plum, ripe for the picking. A body feels he might reach out and touch it if he could but climb a bit higher up into the heavens. So bright does it shine, if the rivers are thawed, a trapper can walk his lines all night long using the light it gives off to show him the way."

Blind Deer watched Kade's face as he spoke. His strong profile and earnest expression revealed his great love for the land and the wilderness. A handsome and noble face, one she fancied she would have been content to grow old beside.

"Maybe we'll see the next Trapper's Moon together. Who knows?" He gave her hips a playful sideways bump with his. "Heck, we'll see many a Trapper's Moon, and the first snow in winter, and the wonder of the Northern lights."

Her heart ached a little more. Kade possessed such optimism, still believing they would somehow be together—somehow she would stay with him and Tucket. But right now, happiness was no longer an emotion upon which she could base her life. She must make him understand.

"I cannot be in your future, Kade. Your path is freedom, mine is responsibility."

"What are you talking about? Did I do or say something to hurt you?"

"No, you do everything right. Too right. Still, I cannot turn my back on my people."

"Is it because of the young man you once knew, before they sent you to St. Louis? You called him your betrothed. Did he let you down? Take another to his bed while you were gone."

"It is true we were to be married one day, when we were older." She smiled, recalling the day they were promised to one another as children. They had laughed, too young to be serious about the ceremony. "Nikota told me he grew to be a strong brave, but he was also one of those who died. I no longer have an obligation to him, only to the others. Besides, everyone I care about dies. I won't let that happen to you."

"So, I don't get any say in the matter? And not everyone you care about has died, not your brothers."

"It is not my fate." What more could she say to convince him?

"It could be. I'm declaring my love for you, and I have mountain man luck enough for the both of us. Surviving the cave-in proves my words. We don't need fate smiling down on us."

"Fate has never smiled on me, Kade. It has laughed cruelly on many occasions, but it never smiles." Her voice sounded bitter even to her own ears.

****

The next morning, Kade awakened first.

120

Remaining silent, he watched Blind Deer as she lay peacefully in the innocence of sleep. The closeness they had shared last night had been more than he'd expected, but far less then he'd desired. At least she hadn't come apart at the seams when he impulsively declared his love for her—she hadn't said it back either—just she couldn't be part of his future. Meaning what? Sometimes a man or woman had to carve out their own future, even if it meant going against nature, or fate, or a mountain standing in the way.

Easing out from under the warm cocoon of blankets—and her nearness—he braved the chill morning air, quickly pulling on his clothes. Then he revived the fire and fed chunks of wood to the hearth. She had repaired his buckskins and fashioned new moccasins for him from the leather kept in the trunk for such needs. She must feel something for him to perform such a personal almost intimate kindness.

One way or another, they had to work this out. He wasn't about to let the best thing in his life slip away without a fight. He'd probably pushed too hard, should have taken things more slowly. But lucky or not, who knew how much time a body had left on this earth.

Besides, he downright loved Blind Deer. The first time he laid eyes on her lying there so small and helpless, then defiant and brave, he knew she was special.

He'd never felt such an overwhelming need to safeguard and care for anything or anybody, other than Maggie of course. Which reminded him, she was still keeping her distance, and the situation weighed heavy on his heart. They had left her food, and from the cabin he'd seen her come and take it, but then she ran back off into the woods. Up until now, he'd been too stove-in to follow after.

Pondering a wagonload of thoughts and unanswered questions, Kade heated water for washing and making tea. Blind Deer stirred, and he glanced over his shoulder. Usually, she was up first, groomed and bright-eyed by the time he saw her. Today she created quite another picture with sleepy eyes and tousled hair—long, enticing hair. Wearing a linen nightshirt, she looked about six years old. Gratefully accepting the capote he handed her, she padded barefoot over to the welcoming warmth of the fire.

"Good morning," Kade greeted. "Thought I'd cook you breakfast for a change before our confab with your brother this morning."

"Thank you. I did not mean to sleep so late, but then it was a most unusual night." She smiled up at him, her expression wistful.

"I'm the one should be thanking you—for the new footwear. They fit perfect. Never had a nicer pair."

"You are welcome. Your old ones smelled so bad, Tucket buried them."

He gave a chuckle picturing his partner shoveling away. "They saw a lot of miles over the last few years. I'm thinking these will see even more. There's hot water when you want it. Just let me know."

She pulled on her own moccasins and ran the porcupine tail hairbrush through her hair before braiding the locks. Then gathering the capote closer, she left the cabin.

Kade began mixing batter to try his hand at making flapjacks. He'd seen Blind Deer do it often enough—how hard could it be?

Moments later, the cabin clouded over with smoke, reeking with the smell of burning oil. Using a towel, Kade waved the dense fog toward the open door. Blind Deer rushed back in to see what was happening.

"Kade, are you all right?"

"Everything is okay," he reassured between fits of coughing, "but breakfast is a might overdone." Wrapping his hand in the towel, he grabbed the handle of the hot smoking pan, hurried out the door, and set it on the porch.

"Tea will be enough." Stifling a laugh, she carefully opened the precious parchment labeled Zodiac extra fine.

He returned, still holding the bedraggled singed towel. "Good choice. Guess I never realized cookin' could be so dangerous. Tucket and I usually stuck to beans and hardtack."

He made two cups of the brew and handed one to Blind Deer. "It'll be shinin' times when we join up with him at rendezvous. I sure hope he's faring well. I don't like he had to go it alone."

"You know there was no choice."

"I do." He appreciated the logic of her words, but the feeling he'd let his partner down wasn't something he'd experienced before, and not something easily quelled. "Still it's a worry."

They sat at the little table, and after a few moments, he had to broach the subject gnawing at his mind like a beaver after the last lodgepole on Earth. "Blind Deer, in the light of day, I want you to look me in the eyes and deny you love me. Or declare there's no hope you ever could."

Her face went pale then flushed as if angry. "I

refuse to discuss this with you, Kade. I told you we cannot be together."

"I know what you told me. I also remember the way you felt in my arms when we kissed, and even now, the look in your eyes belies your words. If you can't stay with me, then I'll go with you."

Lips pressed together in a firm line, she remained mute. He put down his tea, and leaning forward across the little table, kissed her. Her lips softened, but she did not kiss him back. He had to make her understand, had to convince her to trust in him, and believe in a happy future even though so many bad things had happened in her past.

She struggled to her feet. Her breath came in quick little gasps, as if resulting from the kiss and his nearness. "If we are leaving tomorrow, there is much to do." Still wearing the capote over her nightshirt, she picked up her buckskin dress and leggings and held them to her chest. "You should go check the frying pan. It was very hot and may have caught the porch on fire."

Her request seemed groundless, but he took the hint and left. Standing outside, he nudged the pan with the toe of his moccasin revealing a scorched place on the floorboards. Ironically it was kinda shaped like a heart. A memento to mark the love burning in his heart for Blind Deer? Or an omen because his heart was doomed to burn in unending pain.

When he thought he'd waited long enough he stepped back inside the cabin. Blind Deer opened her painted parfleche bags and began filling them with her few possessions. Jumping up, he followed her around the cabin, trying to slow her down, trying to make her talk to him. Every time she put an item in a pouch, he pulled it back out—until in frustration she turned on him in anger.

"Oh, just leave me alone."

This wasn't going at all as he'd planned. In desperation, he tried one more approach. "I changed my mind. We can't leave yet. Maggie is still hiding out in the woods. Today is the first time I feel strong enough to go looking for her."

As soon as the words were uttered he regretted them. Her face crumpled, anguish showing in her eyes. She stormed from the cabin, leaving the door wide open. After a few steps she turned and faced him full on. "What a cruel thing to bring up, McCauley. You know I did not mean to scare dog away."

Regret riding high, he watched as she stumbled over the rocky terrain in the direction of her brother's camp. He opened his mouth to say something to stop her, but he had no idea what words to use. This couldn't be happening. Last night, although amorously stifled, he was the happiest man in the world. And this morning he was sorrier than a bear cub lost in a spring storm.

Blind Deer headed for the wet muddy ground beneath the large trees. The slick soles on her moccasins gave no footing, and she fell on her backside, arms and legs a flailing.

Kade ran out to help. With each effort to get back up, she slid down again, splashing mud around all the more. When she saw him coming, the expression on her face stopped him in his tracks. "I do not need your help."

****

How dare Kade throw up Maggie's absence in her face? She was heartbroken the animal still feared to come home.

Finally gaining purchase, Blind Deer struggled to her feet. The mud slid down the front of her dress and dripped off the fringes. Her leggings and moccasins were thick with the wet earth, and making an abrupt change in direction, she headed for the stream.

Her life kept changing direction too, just as swiftly and frequently.

When she'd been with Sir Reginald and saw the scorched earth and thought her tribe completely wiped out, all hope of going back to the old ways had been eliminated. Yet amidst the keen heartache, there had come the happy possibility of staying with Kade.

Now Nikota came saying some had survived, forcing her to choose between her past and her future. Her heart screamed in pain for what was—and for what could never be. It wasn't Kade's fault for the way he felt, or for what had befallen her people. Or for the fact that none of the alternatives had hope of success. She wanted to run to him and take her place at his side, now and forever. Her feelings for him were powerful, like nothing she'd felt before. But if she didn't try to help her brethren, she couldn't live with herself. And if she couldn't live with herself, she couldn't live with Kade.

Shoving a branch out of her way, she hurried along the path to the water.

As far as McCauley traveling with her, what if her people refused to accept him? He would always be living in peril. The image wouldn't form in her mind. It would never work.

Almost at the river, she grabbed at handfuls of tall grass, folding the reedy stems into a pad. Without stopping, she waded into the water, gasping as the rushing water soaked through the leather covering her feet and legs. When the majority of the mud was loosened and washed away, she stepped out and sat on a rock, using the stiff little bundle of grass to scrub away what remained.

Her buckskins would turn stiff and need working— she should wear them until they dried, an unappealing prospect. Squatting down by the water she washed her face, neck, and arms, welcoming the coldness as it too brought back memories. Her people frequently bathed in cold streams, yet ignorant and not caring about her customs, the missionaries had forced her to bathe in cold water as a punishment. It only made her stronger. Here was another example of her two worlds colliding.

Hearing a sound, she squinted and glanced around. Did someone approach? Had Kade followed her after all? She did not wish to see him. She needed time alone, and to talk again with her brother.

"Kade McCauley," she called, "turn around now, and go back to the cabin."

A bone chilling growl answered her request.

In her haste to get away from Kade, and to clean up, she'd forgotten to approach the stream with caution. A small black bear stood downstream in the middle of the water. Nose in the air, he sniffed in her direction. Although she couldn't see him clearly, judging from the size of the big dark blur, he wasn't fully grown—but big enough to kill her.

She drew her Green River Blade, eased out of the water, and back-stepped the way she'd come. The bear charged up stream, sending sheets of water rooster-tailing out in every direction. Closer now, she could see every detail, and the sight near made her heart stop beating. Turning to seek a means of escape, an unseen rock took her down—face first. She was done for. Raising her head, she caught a glimpse of light-colored fur flashing by from out of the woods. Maggie…

With a blood chilling howl, the dog charged forward, and both animals crashed into one another. Taken by surprise the bear stumbled and slid to a halt. Maggie bit at the huge creature's nose and eyes. The bear swiped a giant paw sideways, catching dog's ear. Brave Maggie stood her ground. Head down, circling as if for the kill, she gave another coyote yowl, and the bear hesitated, but not for long. Blind Deer scrambled to her feet. Knife in one hand a tree branch in the other, she took her place beside Maggie.

Young and inexperienced, the bear seemed confounded by the two-pronged attack. Still mad at Kade, and basically the entire world, Blind Deer gave a war cry of her own, a savage sound, years in the making. The critter turned and ran—Maggie biting at his heels.

"Maggie, dear Maggie. You saved me." Comrades born of war, she called dog by name.

Maggie came unafraid to her side. Blind Deer knelt, threw her arms around the big dog's neck, and buried her face in the familiar fur. Then she examined the dog for wounds. One ear was torn and bleeding, but otherwise she seemed unharmed.

Coyote/dog whined and came to attention. Something or someone was coming, but not the bear. She couldn't see his face clearly, but knew by his outline and way he walked, it was Kade. Maggie ran toward him tail wagging, tongue lolling.

Blind Deer hurried to catch up.

"I heard Maggie howling, as well as a downright frightful scream. Are you both all right?" He bent to examine the dog's ear. "What happened, old girl? That's gonna leave a scar." He stroked her head a few times then straightened. "Blind Deer, what happened to your face?" His fingers shook as he reached out to touch her cheek.

She explained about the bear and about falling down for the second time this morning. "Maggie saved me, Kade. I think she has forgiven me."

Planted firmly between the two of them, Maggie sat guard at their feet, tail thumping as she gazed up at them.

"I think she knows how much you mean to me." His eyes still held a troubled expression.

"I know too, Kade."

****

While Blind Deer washed and treated Maggie's ear, Kade drank a cup of the special *strengthening* tea she brewed for him. He was proud of Maggie for saving Blind Deer, and the new closeness between the two of them came as a relief. Maybe it didn't change things between him and Blind Deer, but it was one less heartache to deal with.

When Maggie was patched up, they headed out. Kade took a few deep breaths. This morning's foray having left him a little lightheaded—he wasn't as strong as he thought. But he wasn't about to show any weakness in front of Blind Deer's brother.

"What's this brother's name again?"

"This one's name is Nikota."

"And you have two more."

"Yes. Somewhere out there. They are Kintama and

Kinnapa. They are the twins, born in a rain storm. Their names mean thunder and lightning. They are true children of the Great Coyote, as they excel at playing tricks. They could always make me laugh. But they are also kind and good at heart."

What would it be like meeting those two? Fond of pranks, and he wouldn't be able to tell them apart. Sounded like a recipe for trouble. "What does Nikota mean?"

"His name means, Refuses-to-Wait. And lucky for my mother he came early to be born, because even as an infant he was large."

Hard to image the huge downright scary man ever being a baby, and Refuses-to-Wait probably still fit his current temperament. Kade walked faster. They were already a might late meeting up with him.

"Hello in camp." Kade gave the usual greeting when approaching another man's site—a good idea to prevent someone throwin' fire or loosing arrows in your direction.

With packs of hides stacked to one side, Nikota sat by the fire, the sun glinting off the war plunder HBC gorget hanging around his neck. Apparently, he'd slept out in the open.

As they drew closer, Blind Deer's brother growled and leapt to his feet, his heated gaze focused upon her face, one hand on the bone hilt of his knife.

"Friend," Kade commanded Maggie, who appeared ready to pounce.

Blind Deer placed a restraining hand on her brother's arm. "It is from a run in with a small bear. Kade would never hurt me."

Nikota relaxed his stance. Kade felt a spark of

happiness knowing Blind Deer understood he would never mean to cause her pain.

"And this is Maggie," Kade added. "She helped chase off old Ephraim."

The expression on Nikota's face went from surprise to stone cold. "She looks like Coyote's sister."

"She does." Blind Deer nodded in agreement. "And owing to her name, I hope you will treat her with respect. Have you any food?" Blind Deer glanced around, and Kade felt sorry again about burning breakfast.

"Does the white man not provide for you?" Nikota's manner and speech held both ridicule and protectiveness.

"Of course. But were we not taught to offer repast to guests?"

With a harrumph, Nikota turned and rummaged around in a parfleche. It was amusing to see the big man giving-in to Blind Deer's reprimand regarding good manners. He offered her a small bag of dried berries. "There is meat in the pot." He nodded toward the kettle hanging over the fire, a stew simmering inside.

As if Blind Deer realized admitting hunger would show weakness on his part, she handed Kade a few berries without his asking. They were sweet, and they were good, and he tried not to wolf them down.

Brother and sister took their place around the fire, and Kade followed their lead.

"My sister and I leave tomorrow. You up to traveling?"

Kade bristled but held back a smart-mouth reply. Maybe he looked worse than he thought, or maybe he just looked as bad as he felt. But he'd survived in the mountains for ten years, and every year out here seemed to count for two in harshness and loneliness. He was good to go.

"More than ready—thanks to Blind Deer. She's been a big help to me ever since we partnered up."

If a staring contest counted as warfare, the battle was on. Nikota had multiple reasons for hating white men, especially one with designs on his sister. Kade figured he would have felt the same way. And to be truthful, deep down, he wasn't without a modicum of resentment for what had happened to his parents. But he tried not to dwell on that part of his past. And living out here, judging a man by his character and his actions until proven otherwise generally worked out best for everybody.

Blind Deer took charge of the situation. Around her brother, her personality seemed more confident and decisive. He was beginning to realize she was a woman with strong opinions, and deep feelings to back them up. He hoped in time some of those feelings would be for him.

"There is more to the story of what happened to our band, Nikota. I need you to tell me the truth." Blind Deer casually chewed on a piece of meat she'd fished out of the pot with a stick, but with back stiff and shoulders squared Kade knew she braced for the news to come.

Nikota studied her for a moment then nodded. "Last year, the HBC came to our village to trade for beaver hides, but the blankets they gave us contained disease. We were struck down, worse than any attack from man or beast. The twins survived because they were over the mountains when the provisions were brought to camp." Nikota's voice sounded fueled by hate.

"The English who brought the goods died too, cursing their Captain because he must have known death rode in their packs. It was the same Captain Sulgrave who searches for you now. Helpless to protect them, I watched my friends and our father die."

Blind Deer's chin quivered, but she stayed strong. "So, to kill the disease you burned the village—and the bodies of those who perished."

"Yes."

"It broke my heart to see our childhood in ashes, bones scattered at random peeking up through the charred memories." One lone tear now cut a path down her cheek.

"I am sorry, my sister. I am glad you were not there to see them die. A nightmare could not have been more horrible. From the youngest to the oldest, there was much suffering. We could not tend the animals, so we set them loose to fend for themselves. Being white, our mother and her longtime friend seemed to fare better for a while as they tended the sick. They saved some, including me, but not themselves."

"What happened to Kinnapa and Kintama? Where are they now?"

"The two had gone over the divide, to the far side of the mountains. They were looking to trade with our brothers the Kootenai—buffalo for salted salmon. They were gone a long time, and when they came back it was too late for them to even say goodbye or to partake in the death ceremonies. Now they lead those few who are left out of the valley, back to the other side where they will live with another Salishan tribe. They will need provisions for the winter. I have hides to trade."

"That is why you're heading for the Siskeedee?" Kade asked.

"Yes. One of the reasons."

"What makes you so sure Sulgrave knew the blankets were deadly?"

"His men discovered they'd only been issued supplies enough for a one-way trip. Their Captain never wanted our trade goods, only the death of my people because we would not let them trap on our land."

Kade figured Nikota's second reason for heading south would be to get revenge on Captain Sulgrave.

Chapter Twelve

Tucket could see better out of his left eye now, as the swelling had gone down, but his left arm felt useless on occasion. Still, he'd successfully defended his rendezvous campsite. And he'd damn-well continue to do so.

Running late, the supply wagons from back East hadn't arrived as yet, and the pressing and bartering of hides hadn't started. Therefore, guarding the plews had been his main concern, causing him sleepless nights, uncomfortable days, and a few nasty altercations.

In the meantime, the HBC boys were crossing swords and throwing punches with any free trapper brave enough to show up, especially one rash enough to show up alone. But he'd held his own against those pork eaters—barely.

As he set about rustling up breakfast, he wondered if this truly would be his last year trapping. The job got harder, the return got less, and from talk around camp, even the High Uinta was getting trapped out.

He knew one thing for sure—he wished Kade and Blind Deer would hurry up and get here. Had Kade gotten worse, or had they met with a band of Blackfoot or Rees? Them Arikara were as deadly as they come. Since he couldn't backtrack to help them or find out how things were going, there was nothing left for it but the praying.

Speaking of which, the Rev. Henry Spalding and Dr. Marcus Whitman had shown up again this year, all the way from New York City. And much to everyone's surprise, they brought their wives along. They were the first white women ever to attend rendezvous.

He didn't especially have anything against psalm singers, but a man endured life in the mountains so's he didn't have anyone telling him what to do, or what to believe in. And while religion was strong medicine, too much of it could be poisonous.

The mountains had always meant freedom and shinin' times. Indeed, things were changin', and not for the better.

****

"The men you sent out ain't nowhere to be found, Captain. Seems they should have been here by now."

Captain Sulgrave had already come to the same conclusion. The elite in Montreal and London didn't realize there was a war going on in the territory, and in regard to this particular situation, he'd made the mistake of not treating it as such either.

The Indian woman and those damnable free trappers were probably on the way here anyway. He should have waited. Now more of his men were missing in action, or more probably dead. Did it really matter? Soon all this would all be just a bad memory. Still, he didn't like losing—for any reason or to anyone. And the reward for the runaway bitch would be helpful to his plans.

"Just concentrate on what's going on here," he ordered. "Get Carson on his feet and moving. He should be able to recognize the two Americans we're after, and the half-breed woman won't be hard to spot.

Let me know immediately when they show up. Until then, keep watch on the other free trappers already here. Dismissed."

As his subordinate went to follow orders, Captain Sulgrave's gaze drifted over the camp. A big one this year, spread-out almost a mile long, following the river. A small city really, where anything could happen— good or evil. Rarely trusting to the good, he was willing to risk the help of the evil.

He spotted Spalding and Whitman—and their wives Narcissa and Eliza. Dispatched by the American Board of Commissioners of Foreign Missions and blinded by the light of God and truth and right, the little group of Protestants was heading for the Northwest to save the world. Or at least one little corner of it. He couldn't care less about the success or failure of their grand intentions, or even the continuation of their lives. As previously planned, they were simply his ticket out of here.

Governor Simpson had volunteered the HBC to escort the religious group west to Vancouver following rendezvous. Once the wagon train was well on its way, Sulgrave intended to cut out and double back, heading for the East Coast and then Europe. He should be long gone before anyone of consequence took note of his disappearance.

With a sigh of resignation, he sallied forth. Although hard to stomach this early in the morning, he supposed he should make an attempt at small talk with the proselytizing do-gooders. Gaining their friendship and trust was integral to his plan.

Chapter Thirteen

The three of them, four if you counted Maggie, were making good time. Nikota rode a few paces behind, ever vigilant, never uttering a word.

For Kade, the past few days spent riding beside Blind Deer meant hour after hour of sweet torture. To have her near, yet beyond reach, was maddening. A condition he endured because any alternative sounded even worse.

As a breeze played with her hair and the sun warmed her lips and cheeks, both elements became the target for his jealousy. He even envied her horse. Without any appreciation, the beast enjoyed the grasp of her firm thighs and the brush of her ankles on its belly.

Someday... Unfortunately, so far, chipping away at her ironclad veneer hadn't worked. She spoke to him politely, but only when necessary.

When they'd first crossed paths, he figured her withdrawn attitude had been from her fear and distrust of him. Now it might be because she feared herself, distrusting the feelings he was convinced she felt for him.

He had to admire her devotion to her tribe though. Wouldn't have expected less from her. And if Blind Deer did agree to abandon her responsibilities and go with him, the decision would always lurk in the shadows. Maybe one day taking form and coming to light between them. But for her to garner supplies and return to the high country would be dangerous. And what would her life be like bound to strangers by loyalty and fading memories of the past rather than by love? She'd just escaped one personal prison and seemed to be heading toward another.

Following after her might still be a possibility, whether she wanted him to or not. But what about Tucket? They were both accustomed to their freedom. And they were partners, with a bond between them strong as in any family. He couldn't just up and leave the man who had taken on the chore and aggravation of raising him.

He glanced over to Blind Deer and caught her watching him. The sadness in her eyes nearly broke his heart. There was no easy answer. Only heavenly intervention or catastrophic circumstance was likely to change the course they each followed. And even at rendezvous, where he'd seen many a curious thing transpire, it seemed highly improbable.

"We should come upon the Green well before sundown. If you like, we can stop along the river to wash up before we reach rendezvous."

"Thank you. I would appreciate doing so." Blind Deer turned her gaze toward the river.

At this particular juncture, the waterway meandered lazily, twisting and turning and spreading out wide. The cottonwood overhanging the water created several private places for bathing. When he halted near a stand of trees, Blind Deer and Nikota reined in too. All three dismounted and rummaged around in their packs.

He chose a spot near the horses and his mule. Blind Deer wandered another twenty yards upstream. Twenty miles away wouldn't be far enough to blur the thought of her naked in the water. Ever vigilant, Nikota picked a spot halfway between the two of them. Kade stripped down and splashed into the water, welcoming the numbing effect.

Maggie ran back and forth along the water's edge, first watching Blind Deer then coming back to where Kade had gone in. Even the poor dog seemed confused by their separation. Maybe when they found Tucket, he could at least convince Blind Deer to come back to them after she did what she could for her people. But come back to what?

If Tucket quit beavering, then he would too, and they would have to come up with some other way to keep body and soul together. A new beginning. Having been a wheelwright, a whaler, and a trapper, Tucket was practiced at changin' jobs. But the very thought scared Kade half to death. Trapping was all he'd ever known.

He floated and fretted, truly concerned about everybody's future including his own.

When the cold soaked in bone deep, he scrambled out of the water to lie in the sun until he was dry enough to dress. Then he sat under a tree, waiting for the woman he loved. Nikota stood guard not far away.

When Blind Deer appeared, the vision of her left him entranced. Her hair, no longer in braids, fell in soft waves around her head and shoulders—the part in the middle now darkened with vermillion. Feathery wisps of the same red hue adorned the corners of her eyes, and a four-strand necklace fashioned from hair pipe beads caressed her throat. She took his breath away.

Gaining his feet, he headed her way, ignoring the disapproving expression Nikota aimed in his direction. "I never thought you could look more beautiful than the night we stood in the moonlight, but I was wrong."

She seemed pleased by the compliment but didn't reply.

"I know your actions are born of a worthy cause, Blind Deer, but none of this makes a bit of sense to me. And no matter what you say, I can't stop loving you."

"You must try, Kade. And you must promise to let me do what needs be done."

"Dangnamit, woman. You're the most stubborn female I ever came across. In fact, you're more stubborn than any mule I ever ran into. And by the way, it would be easier to promise you the moon and the stars than to promise to stop loving you."

"The moon and the stars are a gift no one can give me. But you are the most caring man I have ever known. Please do not ruin my high opinion of you."

How could he argue with that request?

He walked beside her toward her horse and his mule, Maggie and Nikota close behind.

"Let's get going, then," he muttered as they mounted up. "The sun is low now, and it'd be best to arrive before true dark."

****

They crested a small rise, and the scene below was a sight to behold, bringing them to an abrupt halt.

Tipis and tents, bright white against the gathering darkness, dotted the valley below, and smoke from lodges and cooking fires swirled upward, hanging in the air like a great blue-winged beast. Even at this distance, the revelry was palpable, the excitement spurring them back into motion.

Picking up the pace, they crossed the open space surrounding the gathering, and with the smell of food enticing them forward, they rode into camp, the newest objects of interest.

"Where's Nikota?" Kade glanced around for Blind Deer's brother.

"He is master of the shadows. He is not far away."

"Well, you two stay close by," Kade ordered Maggie and Blind Deer.

They made their way through what could easily pass for a small city. Well-worn paths already crisscrossed the encampment, especially around Trader's Row where every gewgaw and foofaraw a man could imagine was available for sale or trade. Although not legal, there were tents hawking hard liquor, while betting games of every sort broke out in the most unlikely places.

The portable hide press stood idle tonight, a gathering place for trappers to jaw about last year's take and this year's price. In contrast, the blacksmith's forge and anvil sang with activity, mending traps, and making fireirons as well as horse shoes.

Dogs barked, babies cried, and Indian children shrieked and played underfoot while grown men—down from the mountains, glad the long winter nights were behind them—danced and drank and cavorted about much like children themselves. Excitement boiled forth from every direction, and somewhere in the distance they heard a mouth harp being played to clapping hands and out of tune voices.

"Maybe we'd better get down and walk."

As if to confirm Kade's suggestion, an isolated pistol shot, fired in enthusiasm rather than anger, went off too close for comfort. Their animals shied to one side, and Maggie started barking. Kade and Blind Deer slid from their mounts, and holding the leads tightly, they headed for the thick of the noise and confusion.

"It could take a while to find Tucket." Blind Deer halted to glance around. "This gathering is much bigger than I ever imagined."

"Tucket will most likely be on the fringes—he likes his peace and quiet. Look for the best campsite. That'll be him."

A commotion up ahead caught Kade's attention. Two men came a stumbling and singing at the top of their lungs. One wore a red derby, the other a Scottish tam. They high-stepped right between him and Blind Deer, both mountain men flushed of face and out of breath, and having the time of their life.

Blind Deer laughed at their antics, and Kade's heart warmed at her happiness. Did she realize what power she wielded over his moods and his feelings? Even now, surrounded by all manner of curiosity, he was satisfied to watch only her.

Standing taller and prouder as he walked at her side, he stole frequent glances in her direction. The fact other men's gazes also followed her passage did not escape his attention. Protectively, he placed his free hand at the small of her back, making sure there was no doubt as to whom she was with.

By the time they wended their way over to the horse camp and temporary livery, it was true dusk. While Blind Deer watched for Tucket, Kade kept glancing around for HBC men. He noticed plenty of them at a distance and was glad now for the growing darkness.

"Are you tired?"

"No, not yet." She shook her head. "I am much too excited to be trail weary."

"Then how about some food?"

"That sounds wonderful. I am near starved."

"Tie your cup to your belt. We can leave the rest of our gear with the mounts. It'll be easier to maneuver around, and we won't go far." He splurged and handed a half-dime to the man who promised to watch her horse and his mule. Their personal possessions should be safe enough temporarily. Thievery at rendezvous was not only frowned upon but was dealt with swiftly—and severely.

In only a few steps, they found a man trading for a finger's width of homemade whiskey. Beside him, an old Indian woman sold venison stew served in small hollowed-out rounds of bread. They bought both.

Sitting on a log, they tore into the food, sharing with Maggie as much as their greedy stomachs would permit. The whiskey, strong enough to blow up a stump, burned Kade's throat and made his eyes water, but the warm glow spreading through his innards was worth the suffering. He stared in amazement as Blind Deer downed her small sampling without batting an eye. His raised brow of surprise prompted an explanation.

"Back at the boarding house, Cook hid a bottle of sherry behind the flour sack in the pantry. I sampled it a few times. When she caught me, instead of slapping me silly, she just laughed. After that, on occasion we shared a tipple, especially after I'd been whipped or locked in the root cellar. For some reason, Cook took pity on me. She even taught me how to bake her famous desserts. I wish we'd had the ingredients at the cabin to make fruit tarts, her specialty and mine.

Hearing new details of how she had been treated in St. Louis revived his anger at what she'd been through. It seemed a wonder she had any goodness or compassion left inside of her at all. The recent events and news of her tribe must surely be wearing on what remained.

Stomachs full, they collected their mounts and gear and headed for the outskirts near the river. Kade recognized Tucket's silhouette right off. The man had a certain way of standing upright while still leaning on his rifle. And his fur hat with the turkey feather sticking out on one side was a dead giveaway.

Maggie's tail went into action as she too spotted Tucket.

"Well damn my eyes." His partner went all smiles as they drew near. "I'm glad to see ya lookin' so fit, Kade. And Blind Deer, the sight of you be a balm to whatever might ail a man. I'd all but given up on the likes of you three." He reached down and gave Maggie a pat, then straightened up slowly.

Kade gave his friend a bear hug and a slap on the back before he noticed Tucket favoring one arm. And even in the vanishing twilight a body couldn't miss the fading bruises ringing his left eye.

"What'd you tangle with, partner?"

"The HBC brigades are harassing the free trappers, and by harassing, I mean beatin' the tar out of thems they catch unawares. It's poor doin's this year, Kade, worse than ever. I been awake near night and day guarding the plews. I'll be glad to have them traded off. I wasn't looking forward to doin' such without ya, but I would have, quick as snowflakes melt in June."

Having said his piece, Tucket retired to one of three stumps he'd collected and set around the fire pit as if awaiting his and Blind Deer's arrival. Two willow backrests also stood nearby. They all sat.

Tucket's camp was orderly and welcoming, the mules picketed nearby. A cut of canvas rigged in the trees gave shelter, and the fire burned small but bright. His 'hawk, knife, and possibles bag were all within arm's reach. His rifle across his lap.

"Where's the HBC horses?"

Tucket related the story of his travels and run in with the Crow.

"Glad they came in handy." Kade nodded staring at the stacks of hides. "When do you figure the tradin' will start?"

"Tomorrow. The supply train just got here yesterday. They came in from the south, kicking up a dust storm on the sage flats. Joe Meek and a few Nez Percés rode out to meet Fitzpatrick—a whoopin' and a hollerin' and a shootin' in the air. It was quite a sight.

"And they had two white women with them, Kade. Waugh... Never heard of such a thing. Even Jim Bridger was surprised."

"Well here's another surprise. Blind Deer's brother showed up."

"I'll be. Didn't know she had one."

"She has three."

"What's the news of your family, gal?"

They told Tucket the situation. He appeared genuinely saddened. "You should stay with us, little gal. You know you're welcome and…" At Blind Deer's determined expression, his partner seemed to lose track of his thought.

"I'm glad you're here now anyway." The sincerity of his words brought a smile back to her face. "This child's been so dang lonely I almost let myself be sweet talked into gettin' hitched. Luckily, I came to my senses before the nuptials, 'cause by Jove my mule was a sight better lookin' than this lively female. A man's got to guard his heart and his purse-strings with equal attention around here."

"You old griz, you'd be lucky any female had her sights set on you."

"You might have a point there." Tucket gave a chuckle and retrieved his pipe from his possibles bag.

They fell into companionable silence, staring at the fire, each left to his own particular imaginings.

****

"Captain, Captain. Carson saw the two free trappers and the Indian woman in camp. The ones massacred our men."

Finally, his chance for revenge and a sweet profit before leaving this life behind. "Excellent. We'll need to act swiftly. Take them alive if possible—we can make an example of them. Nobody crosses the Hudson Bay Company." How hard could it be to overtake two ruffians and a squaw? "Pick three men, fully armed. Then report back here and bring Carson. Make sure he's sober. He's our witness."

A bit later, Sulgrave marched through the camp with his little brigade. The chaos of humanity before him split aside like waves before the bow of a ship. They also closed in again at his back. A lesser man might be fearful because there were many who did not like the HBC or him. But being frightened was the last thing on his mind.

He wanted justice and would have it soon. Unless other free trappers came to the aid of the three he sought, both men and the green-eyed Indian were done for. Tonight, those who cheated the company and stole from others would get a lesson in how the king enacted justice.

Chapter Fourteen

Tucket was on his feet first, rifle at the ready.

Kade took notice of the reason why, and joined him—knife in one hand, the other resting on the Charleville pistol hooked to his belt. Maggie began to growl, hackles rising. "Blind Deer, keep ahold of Maggie."

Grateful for once she did as requested without an argument, Kade could at least put that concern out of his mind as he faced the oncoming group of armed soldiers.

"I'm Captain Sulgrave, and by authority of the British Crown, you are under arrest for the murder of three men under the protection of the HBC. We have a witness to the encounter. And this Indian woman is wanted in St. Louis for thievery." A man stepped forward at Sulgrave's signal, and then waved the wanted poster for all to see.

"You ain't got no authority here, other than with your own men," Tucket pointed out. "And so far you ain't been doin' a very good job of keepin' them under control."

"And it was self-defense, not murder," Kade corrected. "Your men fired first, and they're guilty of kidnapping this woman." He snatched the missive, perused it, crumpled it, and threw it in the fire. "I don't care what your piece of paper says, or whose picture

149

you got on it, she's done nothing wrong, and she stays with us."

Sulgrave's gaze narrowed, and he stared at Blind Deer with more interest than Kade appreciated. "Just your word against ours, free trapper, and you're outnumbered—unless someone amongst this rabble has the ill-fated notion to stand with you." The Captain leisurely glanced around. The crowd fell silent and eased back a step or two. Not one person came forward to help.

Kade gave Tucket a quick study trying to discern what he might be thinking. They'd seen their way through skirmishes before, and he knew they could fight off most of the armed men, but the end-result sounded unappealing—dead or captured. If they went peaceable, they might have a chance to get away later without injury to anyone.

But what about Blind Deer? She'd be at the mercy of the HBC again, and in the hands of this man. Sulgrave had lifeless eyes, like a snake's, and a hard sneer of a mouth to go with them. Kade would die before he'd let this devil's son touch her.

In the darkness behind their camp, the bushes gave the faintest rustle. Out of the shadows stepped Nikota and two other braves—bows up, arrows nocked, and deadly expressions on their painted faces. They were a beautiful sight.

The group of bystanders gave a collective gasp, and the men with Captain Sulgrave eyed one another as if to bolster their own courage.

The two men with Nikota looked exactly alike. Apparently Kinnapa and Kintama had arrived. Kade was about to breathe a sigh of relief, until Nikota issued, in his native tongue, what sounded like a deadly warning. The brave sought revenge, and who could blame him. But if he killed Sulgrave, he'd pay with his life. A standoff would be better.

Blind Deer seemed to come to the same conclusion. A warrior at heart, she picked up Tucket's tomahawk and took a stand between her brothers and the HBC men. A hush fell over the entire camp, and the tension in the air couldn't have been greater.

The expression on Captain Sulgrave's face slid from calculating to demonic. He wasn't going to give up without a fight.

No longer having the advantage, and endowed with a modicum of decency, the other HBC men didn't appear too anxious to open fire unprovoked. Sulgrave noticed that truth too. "You will hold at the ready," he barked, bring the soldiers to attention. "And you—" Sulgrave pointed a finger at Tucket. "—You and your stinking little band of misfits will surrender now or bear the consequences."

Kade stepped forward. "Take me and leave the others alone. You have no quarrel with them." He heard Blind Deer's sharp intake of breath and prayed she'd hold her tongue and position.

Sulgrave seemed to consider the idea. "A foolishly noble offer, but I'm afraid it won't do. Surprisingly, the woman is worth more than the two of you put together. We will be relieving you of your hides as well."

There seemed no reasoning with Sulgrave, and no mercy in his soul.

As if petrified, they all mutely stood their ground— Kade could almost hear time ticking away. Heart pounding, he prayed no one would make an untoward move or fire an unintentional shot, setting off a blood bath.

Out of the dead silence, the wail of bagpipes split the night. The hairs at the nape of his neck stood on end, and the eerie sound grew louder as a lone piper drew near. Two men followed. One was short, wearing a cape and top hat. The other one, much larger, leaned upon a cane. Unable to resist, even Sulgrave turned toward the commotion. A moment later, he removed his hat and grabbed at his hair as if wishing to tear it from his head in anger.

The short man in the tall hat seemed to be in charge, and unafraid of the Captain. "Sulgrave, what is the meaning of this?"

"These two free trappers killed several of my men, and I am arresting them. There is also a warrant out for the Indian woman."

"It isn't true." Before he could stop her, Blind Deer stepped forward. "The HBC men took me prisoner, and these men saved me. It was a fair battle."

"Bless my soul, is that you Blind Deer?" The taller man pushed forward, coming to stand before her. "I was hoping to find you here, young lady, but not under these circumstances." The man's expression darkened as he turned to face the Captain. "By order of King William, this woman is under my protection. You will cease and desist any hostile action and leave her and her friends in peace."

"Sir Reginald." Blind Deer reached out to the man. "My heart rejoices at your recovery. And you've come to my rescue yet again. I never stole anything, I promise you."

"I believe you, child. When I saw the sketch being

bandied around at the fort, I knew it was a ruse. No doubt perpetrated out of spite by the Reverend and his wife. If you were arrested and in prison, no one would believe your accusations against them and their cruelty. Another crime to add to their list of offenses. They shall be dealt with."

"I'm Governor Simpson." The shorter man in top hat and cape stepped forward, introducing himself. "On behalf of the Hudson Bay Company, Northern division, I apologize for this inconvenience. Captain...to my tent immediately."

"This isn't over." Sulgrave snarled out the threat as he left, signaling his men to disband.

"On that you are correct, Captain. This is not over by a longshot." The Governor appeared red-faced with anger as he spoke to Kade and Blind Deer. "You have my word I will get to the bottom of this."

Blind Deer's brothers didn't look convinced.

"There is more to the story," Kade put in, addressing the government official. If they had any hope of Nikota not taking matters into his own hands, the tale of what happened to Blind Deer's tribe needed to be told to this man.

"I am willing to listen to all accusations. And again, appropriate punishment will be served. Apparently, it has been a long time coming. But the hour is late. See me in the morning, young man. We will take your official statement then."

Their curiosity waning, the bystanders dispersed, talking and speculating amongst themselves.

Chapter Fifteen

The Governor left, but Sir Reginald stayed behind.

"Welcome to rendezvous, Kade." Tucket's sarcastic comment was followed by him reaching for the jug of stump blower. "After looking down the bore of those English rifles, I could use a little something to bolster my spirits."

"I'm with you there, partner. Pass it over." Kade dropped down onto the willow backrest closest to the fire and took a long pull on the jug. Blind Deer continued to speak with the man who had come to her defense. Although curious as a cat, Kade figured to give her some privacy. She would be safe enough with her brothers, Tucket, and himself at hand.

"Who be all those Indian fellas, and that old toff?"

From the bits and pieces of Blind Deer's story, recanted to him while he was in and out of consciousness, Kade figured out who the fancy Englishman must be, and he relayed the information to his partner.

"You mean for sure she won't be stayin' on with us?" Tucket appeared as brokenhearted as Kade felt.

"I reckon not. I was hoping to marry her, Tucket. I have never felt this way for any women I ever met. It'll be poor doin's when she's gone. No more shinin' times. I'm not sure I can face another winter without her."

"I'm sorry to hear it, son. Either way, with or

without her, I'm not sure I can face another winter in them Stony Mountains myself."

"You been saying such for years," Kade accused.

"I mean it this time. I'm tired of fighting the British, and the price of plews keeps a droppin' while the price of supplies rises faster than a feather in a wind storm. No profit to be made. I gotta start lookin' after my retirement years."

Kade felt his heart being squeezed from both sides. He was about to lose the woman he loved and his partner in the only livelihood he'd ever known. "You got a few more years left in you for floatin' your stick."

"The beaver are just about played out. I seen it happen with the whales, and it'll happen to those poor critters too."

"Then how about the buffalo. There's money to be made there."

"Nope. My soul can't take any more bruises. Killin' your share for eatin' or feedin' folks is one thing. But they're a slaughterin' those magnificent critters just for the skin, lettin' the rest go to rot."

Kade gave a mighty sigh. "I hear ya. Then what the devil are we gonna do? Trapping's all I know."

"All ya know right now. Don't mean ya can't learn something new. We could pilot some of the wagons heading to Oregon. Or we could just go ourselves and stake a claim before it gets too crowded out there too."

"And do what, become farmers?"

"Farmin' ain't nothin' to be ashamed of. Or maybe we could open a tradin' post on the shore. I'm handy with a boat and could do some netting. Salted fish is a good seller for the land voyagers. And your Pa was a cobbler—anywhere you go folks be needin' shoes. I know for a fact you're still draggin' around some of his tools. I'm handy at whittling. I can make you your wooden lasts for formin' the shoes."

The idea started to sound like a possibility. If he had to go on without Blind Deer, starting something new to occupy his mind and body would help keep him from pining away for her.

He glanced over at Tucket. His friend puffed away on his favorite pipe, the one carved from the piece of catlinite they'd traded for two years ago. Kade supposed Tucket was looking a might older lately, and after his own recent injuries, Kade was feeling older himself. Maybe a new beginning was just the thing. In truth, for the long haul, they could both use a future of a more genteel nature.

"Well, I'm sure not looking forward to another winter of wading up to my crotch in freezing river water. Or battling the shut-in crazies either. It's a deal, partner. We'll head west together."

****

"I am joyful you have recovered so well, Sir Reginald."

"Without you nursing me back to Fort Hall, I'm not sure I could have made it." His eyes brightened in curiosity as he took in Nikota, Kinnapa, and Kintama.

"You fought hard to get there," Blind Deer praised. "But why are you here? You should still be resting."

"The sketch of you came to my attention as it circulated around the fort, along with the ugly messenger they sent to find you. I was hoping to track you down before anyone else could. You mentioned the possibility of coming to this year's regalia, and when the Governor and an HBC contingency from Fort Elise stopped off at Fort Hall, heading this way, I demanded an escort."

"So, you are a great adventurer after all, Lord Seton. Did you get to stay in a tipi?" She remembered his list of things he'd wished to accomplish out West.

"I did indeed. A bit of a smoky proposition at times, but quite comfortable and warm. Although I must admit, I am spoiled and much prefer the marquee for long term use."

"And did you shoot a grizzly bear in honor of Hugh Glass?" She thought of her and Maggie's run in with the small black bear. She wouldn't want to face down a grizzly.

"Good heavens no," he chuckled. "We saw a fantastic sow at a distance. Her size and magnificence were beyond my imagining. But with two cubs at her side, she appeared in a bit of a foul mood, so we thought discretion the better part of honor."

"A wise choice." She grinned back at him.

"Now you must introduce me to these stalwart lads."

"This is my brother, Nikota."

"We are all her brothers," piped up Kinnapa and Kintama in unison.

"Amazing. It's an honor to meet you. Good show taking a stand against Captain Sulgrave. He's an unsavory man to say the least. And I'm so glad you found your family, Blind Deer."

Although happy to see her brothers, she explained to Lord Seton the news was not good, emphasizing the part Captain Sulgrave had played in the death of her clan.

"So, this is the story yet to be told. Oh, my poor

child. You go from the frying pan to the fire, do you not? This won't stand. I will inform Major Simpson of what Sulgrave did to your people. And we shall call off that ruffian bounty hunter and clear your name here as well as with the law in St. Louis. You have my promise. You are no longer a fugitive."

"He must die." Nikota stepped forward, hate gleaming in his eyes.

"Now listen, young man. Your cause may be worth dying for, but he is not. You must stay alive, for the sake of your sister and brothers. I give you my word, he will pay for his evil machinations."

Blind Deer placed a restraining hand on Nikota's arm. He was a changed man, no longer the gentle being she knew growing up—he was scarred—on the outside and the inside. And rightfully so. "Please listen to him, brother. He is a man of honor. If you kill the HBC man, they will kill you, and I cannot lose you after finally finding you. We are all who are left to carry on the old ways of our tribe."

With the arrival of Kinnapa and Kintama had come more bad news, the final blow. The few remaining members of her band had been too sick to survive the trek over the mountains to their tribal cousins. They too were gone—all of them gone forever.

Much had changed in the years she'd been held captive back East. The land was no longer a wilderness. There were permanent trails made by white men, trails so familiar they were depicted on maps. The buffalo had moved to new grounds, and the beaver grew sparse. This was no longer the land of her people, and now another part of her dream was lost. With each revelation, her place in the world became more uncertain. She had no place to return to. And except for her brothers, no one to travel with into the future.

"I'm sorry about your troubles." Sir Reginald's voice held genuine sorrow. "What will you do now? If I may assist you in any manner you must allow me to do so."

"You have been very kind and generous. To clear my name is all I ask. I must find my own path now."

"You are a remarkable woman, Blind Deer." As if she were a great lady, Lord Seton took her hand and bent to reverently kiss the top. "I will be sure King William knows the name of the brave Salish woman who came to the aid of this old wanderer." He glanced over his shoulder to where Kade and Tucket sat talking.

"I see you have made new friends since we parted. The younger one defended you bravely. I think he must care very deeply for you. And you for him."

Was it so obvious? Her cheeks felt flushed, and try as she might, she couldn't help smiling at Sir Reginald's assumption.

"Well, lads, I'm proud to have met you." Reaching in his pocket, Lord Seaton pulled out several gold coins. He gave one to each Kinnapa and Kintama. Whooping with great enthusiasm, they danced in joy. He handed the rest to Blind Deer.

Nikota stood by, stoic and silent.

Unpinning a war medal from his lapel, Sir Reginald handed this to her oldest brother. "You are a true warrior. I know you will take good care of her for me."

"I will try. She has a mind of her own."

The older man gave a little bark of laughter. "That she does."

159

Nikota handed Sir Reginald his Missouri war axe, the handle decorated with feathers and beads. "Do not forget your promise. The death of my people must be avenged. If I hear otherwise, I will come back for this."

Lord Seton gave a curt bow of acknowledgement to both the gift and the threat. "I understand. Good night then." Turning, and with a salute to Kade and Tucket, he took his leave.

Blind Deer fondly studied her brothers as the two younger ones drew closer to examine Nikota's war medal. They would be happy living off the land, taking hides and trading for supplies, a good life for three young, healthy braves—but no life for her. She could go to live with a tribe not of her ancestors, but it would be a difficult life. She would be given the hardest tasks, and most likely married off to someone she did not know and did not love.

Her mind was troubled, her thoughts torn in many directions. Seeking calm, she stepped away into the darkness and squinted up at the stars. What about Kade's offer? She held deep feelings for him, born out of love, not the fear of being alone. But she had refused all his offers. Perhaps he did not even want her anymore, or worse would now take her out of pity.

A hand touched her shoulder. Spinning around, she came face to face with the man who seemed her whole world.

"I heard what your brothers told you. And while I'm sorry for what you've lost, there is no excuse now for you not to come with me, Blind Deer. Tucket and I are a headin' for the West Coast. We're selling out—no more trapping. With this year's profit we aim to open up a trading post. He knows the ocean for fishing, and

I'm going to try my hand at cobbling. Maybe you could make and sell those fancy cakes you were telling me about."

Her heart picked up speed—he still wanted her. But what was all this about heading west and starting over? Fishing and shoeing people and baking confections. Now her head was spinning with all these new ideas.

"Well say something." Disappointment showed on his face. "Just stay put. Don't you dare go anywhere." He turned and hurried off before she could bid him stay.

Reaching out, she was about to call him back when Nikota stepped up beside her.

"Let him go, sister. If he really wants you he will come back."

"I love him, Nikota, but I am caught between two worlds."

"You always have been." He put his arm across her shoulders and gave her a hug. "You are much like our mother. She was brave enough to leave her world and become one of us. Maybe now it is time for you to leave behind how you grew up and return to her world. You have her spirit to learn and explore. You could do worse than the white man, Kade. He is resourceful, and for a dogface not too ugly."

This brought a smile.

"But I would have to kill him if he ever hurt you."

She knew this was not an idle threat, still her smile broadened at his concern. "I will be sure to tell him so. Although the way you scowl at him, I have a feeling he already knows. And I will never forget how I was raised, or how we were happy together in the old days."

"That is good. But you must make new memories too, ones to make you just as happy. Go and be free. Wherever you are, we will find you. Now I'd best follow our brothers." He nodded in the directions of the twins. "With money to spend they will surely find trouble at a good price."

****

Tucket leaped up and grabbed ahold of Kade as he came tearing through their camp. "Where you off to in such a hurry?"

"Blind Deer still won't say yes to coming with us to Oregon."

"Well that's darn foolishness. I never see'd two people more fit for one another than you and Blind Deer. You can't be allowin' this to happen, Kade."

Maggie gazed up at the two of them, her eyes troubled as if such an idea upset her too.

"Well that's what I'm aiming to do, old man, if you get out of my way. When we passed through Trader's Row, I saw a few foofaraws and whatnots need buyin'."

"If you're settin' your trap for love, better bait it with your heart and not your brainpan."

Kade nodded and took off.

Tucket gave a laugh and shook his head. He'd never seen young Kade in such a lather. It truly must be love. He thought back to when he was that age and chasing after a pretty girl was all he could think on. Now he just hoped to find a peaceful place to sit and smoke his pipe while watching the sunset. Of course, if a good woman came his way in the new land, he'd be thankful.

And speaking of sittin' and smokin'—he retrieved his pipe and squatted down on his favorite stump. A loud blubbering sound of flatulence followed, sending him leaping back onto his feet. Turning around, he found a limp buffalo bladder on the stump, sewn up with sinew, and filled with the last bit of remaining air. In the woods he heard laughter and saw what he thought were Kinnapa and Kintama running off into the night, Nikota not far behind.

Consarn it, those two were the most mischievous Indians he'd ever crossed trail with. He knocked the offending item off the stump, then sat and filled his pipe with 'baccy. As he was about to light up, Blind Deer came and took to another stump.

Maggie wandered over, sat down, and leaned against her thigh.

"What's this crazy talk I hear about you quitin' us," Tucket asked point blank. "I've know'd young Kade nearly all his life, and I ain't never seen him happier than when you're by his side."

"Where is he?" she asked, apparently disinclined to discuss the matter.

"He'll be back momentarily. Here, have some jug," Tucket offered. "You look a might weak kneed."

She shook her head no. "Are you trying to lead me astray, Tucket?"

"No, gal. I'm a tryin' to help show you the way back home." He puffed on his pipe, leaving her to her thoughts.

****

"By hell, Governor Simpson, what in damnation are you're doing here? And who is this English peacock you deemed to drag along?" Bordering on the brink of his escape to freedom, Captain Sulgrave dared to address his superior with all the years of hate and disrespect he harbored for the man.

"The tallies at Fort Elise present a problem, Captain." Issuing a statement of his own, the Governor ignored the questions. "The discrepancies date back months, even years. It's your responsibility, and I want answers. And this *peacock* is a decorated war hero, who has informed me you traded blankets carrying deadly disease to the Flathead tribe. You killed hundreds of innocent Indians."

"None of these savages are innocent. And those particular ones were getting in the way."

"Then how about your own men, several of whom you also killed in the process. Were they expendable too?"

So, his little deception had come to light. Things were going from bad to worse. "Step aside, old man. Now you're in my way too, and I have packing to do."

"You won't need much. There'll be no gallivanting off to Vancouver or anyplace else, other than Montreal for your court martial."

As blind rage rushed to the forefront, Sulgrave felt as if his head might explode. Simpson had ruined everything, all his plans gone for naught. He leaped at the man, arms outstretched, hands reaching to throttle his scrawny throat.

Lord Seton stepped forward, landing a right cross on Sulgrave's jaw. Taken by surprise, he staggered backward. Then Sir Reginald opened the door and roughly pushed him into the hands of the HBC soldiers waiting to take him into custody. Blows rained down on the Captain from all directions. Apparently, news of how he'd betrayed his men, sending them to their painful death, had already made the rounds.

His chances of reaching Montreal alive were fading fast.

****

When Kade returned, Blind Deer cautiously gained her feet. The grin he wore pleased her yet made her suspicious of his intent.

"Come with me." He took her hand and led her a few steps to the side and away from the light of the fire.

Tucket reached down to pet Maggie, keeping her from following after them.

In the darkness, the air smelled sweet and refreshing, making the world feel somehow hopeful.

"Here." Kade held something out to her. "Take it. It's a present whether you go with me or not."

Again he offered her free choice, the most precious of gifts, one he had given her when first they met. Examining the object more closely, so light and delicate in her hands, she discovered it was a red velvet rose.

"Like my love for you, it will never die. And you won't have to feel guilty for having picked it."

His words touched her heart as softly as she touched the petals of the rose. She couldn't believe he remembered the hill and the flower she'd picked when they'd stayed at the cabin.

"It looks so real. I can almost smell its fragrance." How had she ever believed she could so easily leave this man? She never wanted to be without him and was about to tell him so.

"Oh, there's one more thing. Close your eyes."

Holding back her words, and showing complete trust in him, she did as Kade requested. His fingertips grazed her cheek, then something cool resided on the sides of her face.

"Take a look."

Blind Deer opened her eyes and gasped, stunned by the transformation of her surroundings. Kade had found her a pair of wire spectacles. Her mother had spoken of such wonders. The incredible new world encircled her in crackling clarity.

Gazing up at the night sky left her dizzy and overwhelmed as she saw what before had been but a dream. "You have given me the moon and stars." About to lose her balance she reached out, and Kade was there to steady her. Then, as if her ancestors shared her happiness and condoned the new path she had chosen, a shooting star crossed the heavens. The sign from above filled her heart with joy.

"Go or stay, Blind Deer. It's your decision. I won't try to stop you. At least now you can see where it is you're going." He made light of the situation, but she heard the sadness in his voice.

"Thank you for giving me this beautiful new world. I see not only where I'm going, but what I am meant to be."

"And what is that, Blind Deer?"

She threw her arms around his neck. He held her so tightly she could feel his heart beating against her chest and knew he must feel her heart beating just as hard against his.

"No matter where we are, or how we make our living, I am meant to be the woman in your arms, Kade. When February comes again, and the earth is bathed in the glow of a Trapper's Moon, I will be with you."

He buried his face in the crook of her neck and whispered in her ear. "Then you'll be my wintertime love too—and that means forever."

Glossary of Terms

Some of the following terms, while typical of the day, are now considered offensive, and do not reflect the author's mindset. Also, while trapping was a way of life in the 1800s, the author does not condone trapping of any kind (other than live trapping for rescue efforts).

Booshway—The leader of a party of mountain men. The word comes from the French *bourgeois*, used by the voyageurs.

Boudins—A buffalo gut containing chyme, which was cut into lengths about 24 inches long and roasted before a fire until crisp and sizzling.

Bug's Boys—Slang name for Blackfoot Indians meaning sons of Beelzebub which turned into Bub's Boys and then Bug's Boys.

Catlinite—Pipestone used for carvings, especially pipes.

Capote—A long coat made from wool trade blankets, usually with a hood.

Child and hos—Words for expressing self as in this child/hos ain't never seen such doin's.

Dogface—Used by Native Americans of various nations for fur trappers, mountain men, or white men in general who wore any facial hair, especially a beard.

Doin's—An event or experience, as in "That rendezvous was some fine doin's."

Ephraim—Mountain man term for grizzly bear, usually Old Ephraim.

Fachan—Scottish ogre.

Gorget—Usually the French pronunciation, the word

means a small piece of armor protecting the throat—often decorative, tied around the neck with leather or cord.

Hole—A valley such as Brown's Hole and Pierre's Hole.

Kentucky long rifle—The long rifle, also known as longrifle, Kentucky rifle, or Pennsylvania rifle, one of the first to use rifling vs smoothbore. Although the Hawken rifle is more famous, the majority of mountain men carried other types of firearms.

Kinnikinick—Tobacco and dried sumac leaves, bark, other natural elements.

Lasts—wooden molds (forms) around which shoes are built.

Made beaver—A dried beaver pelt, usually scraped and stretched, ready to be bundled. Beaver pelts were folded and pressed. On average it took sixty pelts to make a ninety-pound pack.

Painter—a corruption of the word panther. A cougar or mountain lion.

Park—a big valley such a South Park, similar to Hole.

Plews—Beaver hides.

Peetrified—In 1807-08, John Colter explored the area now known as Yellowstone National Park, and astonishing tales of geysers and petrified trees soon followed. This was a frequent distortion of the word.

Parfleche—A hide, especially a buffalo's hide, dried by being stretched on a frame after the hair has been removed and painted.

Pemmican—Used by Indians and mountain men. Food made by mixing powdered jerky with dried berries, wild peppermint, and hot tallow, then packed and stored in skin or gut bags. This is a high energy survival food.

Plews—Term for beaver hides.

Poor bull from fat cow—To know good times from bad, "Them days war Poor Bull for sure."

Possibles—The personal property of the mountain man. Such items as a bullet mold, an awl, knives, a tin cup, his buffalo robe or a blanket capote, his pipe and tobacco, flint and steel, sometimes a small sheet-metal fry-pan, and other accouterments he considered necessary. Firearms were considered *pieces* or guns and not possibles.

Possibles bag—The bag in which the mountain man carried his possibles. Everything from pipe and tobacco to his patches and balls. What could not be carried in the bag were hung on the shoulder strap. Shooting needs were given first priority and kept where they could be found with ease and speed.

Pilgrim—Usually immigrants, people moving west. The term was also sometimes used by the mountain men to mean any man new to the fur trade.

Pull foot—To turn tail and run.

Siksika—Another name for the Blackfoot Indians.

Siskeedee-Agie—Local term for the Green river.

Shining—To shine means to be extra good at something. Thems was shinin' times.

Shining Mountains—An early name for the Rocky Mountains, also called the Stony Mountains.

Short starter—To load a muzzle loader you seat the ball a "short" way down the barrel before using a ramrod.

Snow eater—A chinook wind quickly melting snow.

Sprue—Is the little bump on a lead ball produced when

it is cast.

Tanglefoot—Whiskey.

There go horse and beaver—Meaning to lose everything you owned or have with you.

Throw smoke—To shoot a firearm.

Trace—A trail.

Waugh or Wagh—An exclamation of great emotion, used by both Mountain Men and Indians. Usually denoting surprise, sometimes good, sometimes bad. It is believed to have originated from the sound made by a bear when surprised.

Westerin''—Heading even farther into the frontier all the way to the Pacific Northwest territory, now Oregon.

Whatever way your stick floats—When trapping, a stick was attached to the trap so you could find it. This was an expression similar to *whatever floats your boat*.

A word about the author…

Gini Rifkin writes adventurous romance. Her settings include the American West, Medieval England, Victorian England, and contemporary fantasy. When not reading or writing, she has the privilege of caring for a menagerie of abandoned animals, including ducks, geese, rabbits, goats, donkeys, and cats. Born in Illinois, she was raised by two terrific parents and one very special older sister. When struck by wanderlust, she moved to Colorado and met her husband Gary. They shared the journey for 30 years, spending vacations canoeing, doing Mountain Man reenacting, and traveling around this great country. Although Gary has passed on, he left her with the skills to soldier on alone, and a little bit of him lives on in every hero she creates. Her writing keeps her hungry to learn new things, and she considers family and friends her most treasured of gifts.

http://ginirifkin.blogspot.com

~

Other books by Gini Rifkin

THE DRAGON AND THE ROSE
LADY GALLANT
IRON HEART
SPECIAL DELIVERY
VICTORIAN DREAM
A COWBOY'S FATE,
SOLACE
BLISS
PORTENCE
COWBOYS, CATTLE, AND CUTTHROATS